THAT WAS

SARAYU SRIVATSA

PLATYPUS PRESS, ENGLAND

First published by Platypus Press (UK), 2021

978-1-913007-14-0 (PAPERBACK)
Catalogue no. PP0035

A CIP record for this book is available from the British Library.

Set in 10/14pt Bergamo Pro, FontSite Inc.
Cover and typesetting by Peter Barnfather
Edited by Michelle Tudor

Printed and bound by Clays Ltd, Elcograf S.p.A.

MIX
Paper from responsible sources
FSC www.fsc.org
FSC® C018072

for Rosa, Lola, Tara

That was an innocent country:

There dying would only be a trek to sleep
Or waking through tall mirrors of a dream:
In spite of which all were afraid to die.

– Dom Moraes

Prologue

My memory, like an ant, stops at each hurdle and drifts down a less difficult path. Unsurprisingly, I don't recall much of my childhood, except for a vague memory—a dream within a dream—of lying beneath an apple tree, sunlight trickling through the stencilled leaves, the grass so lush I could taste its wetness, the breeze crisp-cool on my face, and around us, our very own flowers of paradise.

Someone held my hand. Was it my brother? I don't recall. I don't remember my father, either. I have a faded memory of my mother—like a well worn black-and-white photograph; were her eyes, like mine, a deep grey?

My strongest memory is of the older, congested area in Bombay. It had a time-worn smell: of mouldy buildings, of shop walls soiled over the years, of roadside markets that smelled of recent migration, of chlorinated water, of pungent cooking and sharp kerosene, and amidst this patchwork of smells, the fragrance of flowers and incense that rose from the mosque and the temple, the sound of a hundred radios spilling

Bollywood music, and in between the chanting from the temple, the cry from the minaret. The mullah's call reminded me of a faraway place. The wind was different there, sharp and cold. A willow tree sighed in the breeze and birds drifted on taut wings.

I now lived with my uncle and his wife. He was not my real uncle, though, he was my father's childhood friend. They had lived in the same village, but I didn't know its name or where it was. Every time I asked him about my father, his eyes froze and, with pursed lips, he bent his head as though in prayer. 'You are our dear daughter,' is all he uttered.

The gold locket I wore on a chain around my neck, the shape of a teardrop, had belonged to my mother, my aunt had told me. Besides me, it was the only other thing that had belonged to her, and each time I touched it, which was often, I felt as though I were touching my mother.

My uncle is a Kashmiri. He is a handsome man: tall and lean, with peach-coloured skin and grey eyes. His parents died in an accident, and he moved to Bombay when he was just sixteen. This was all that he had told me. My aunt is short and stout. She is from the south, her skin the colour of dusk. Her long, black hair had greyed here and there, and her eyes were always uneasy. No one ever accused her of any wrongdoing, but her thoughts did. She imagined that others could read them, that they could hear her think, and this made her anxious.

My uncle and aunt were different from one another, both in demeanour and temperament: my uncle was undaunted,

were soft, much softer than any wool he had seen before. So, when he returned, he did so with many Persian craftsmen. They made socks from the soft wool of these goats. 'Pashm means wool in Persian,' my uncle had said. The Sufi called the wool pashmina. He presented a pair of these fine socks to Zain-ul-Abidin, the king of Kashmir, and the king was so fascinated with them that he started making them in his own kingdom.

After him, Akbar, the Mughal Emperor, set up factories to produce pashmina shawls; they were embroidered with Persian motifs. Akbar's son, Jahangir, wrote in his book that pashmina was his favourite cloth. Later, the Mughals established trade routes to sell the fine woollen cloth. They reached Europe and became fashionable. The French monarch, Napoleon Bonaparte, bought a pashmina shawl for his wife, Joséphine. She was so happy with it that she decided to buy a hundred more, making it desirable throughout Europe. It was the Europeans who called pashmina cashmere because it came from Kashmir. My uncle told me that in those times, pashmina was shipped to America, England, Europe, China, and Japan. The English were so impressed with this fine wool that they tried to replicate it themselves but never succeeded. It was only later that cloth similar to pashmina was developed in Scotland; they named it Paisley after the city it was made in.

Another of my uncle's stories was about chiru, the Tibetan antelope. 'The chiru is home to the botfly,' he told me. In warm weather, these flies burrowed deep into the antelope's skin to lay their eggs. Around this time, the chiru began to shed its winter coat and, to rid itself of the botfly, rubbed against bushes and shrubs—traditionally, this is where the weavers collected the wool. This wool was called shahtoosh, and it was so fine that one and a half yards of the fabric could be passed through a single finger-ring.

My uncle playfully called me his little chiru.

Kyoto, 1991

At the beginning of each month, a parcel and a letter would arrive from Tokyo for my uncle. It contained small, neatly wrapped items for my aunt and me: a scarf, a brooch, hair clips, good luck charms, amulets, and so on. When I asked my uncle who they were from, he wouldn't tell me. But my aunt chuckled and said, 'They're from S-san, his Japanese girlfriend.' Once, I asked my uncle for S-san's address so I could send her a letter to thank her for the precious gifts. My uncle didn't give it to me. I waited for the parcel every month and wrote letters to the mysterious S-san and stored them in a box. Soon these letters became a diary of sorts. They contained details about my everyday life. I confided in her; it was as though she was my mother. *Perhaps, one day, I will meet you*, I wrote. It was not possible, I knew, and yet I hoped.

On one trip to Japan, my uncle returned with a bonsai plant—a desert rose with pink flowers. He had hidden it in his suitcase. My aunt put it on the terrace beside the collection of ceramic pots and bowls she had bought from various shops and exhibitions. When it grew, she repotted it in a large terracotta urn. 'It's becoming arthritic, it has to grow,' she reasoned. It is now taller than me, but on the day my uncle had bought it, it was only a foot high, its knotted roots wrapped in mud and wires, a discarded plastic-pouch, and covered with a three-week-old Japanese newspaper that still smelled of ink.

My aunt resolved that it was a sacred plant, as sacred as the Hindu Tulsi, and every new moon she offered prayers to it. The plant grew, and its pink blossoms gave off a sweet scent that laced the night air.

Briefly, she was confined to bed; her bones also knotted with arthritis. So, on the next new moon, as she would have done, I lit a lamp next to the desert rose, looked up at the dark sky, and prayed to keep her well. Then I switched on the stereo and played The Beatles' "A Hard Day's Night" loudly, since, like my aunt, I wouldn't sing sacred songs.

Afterwards, I tidied my desk. My bed was strewn with old letters and cards and thank you notes to S-san, sketches, photographs, paltry mementoes, and small notepads in which I had jotted important matters, recorded trivialities. But those were merely reminders, remembrances, not memories. Where had my father gone? What had happened to my mother? Whose hand was it that held mine beneath the apple tree?

I don't remember much, but I do recall Ojiisan and Obaasan. And of course, Yasunari. He was Shigeru Hara's son and lived with them in Kyoto since his parents had moved to Tokyo.

On one of his trips to Japan, my uncle had taken me to visit their house. I stayed with them for several weeks—my fondest memories still.

* * *

There was a strong wind during my first night, and the next morning, the garden below was covered with nuts. I lay under the ginkgo tree and watched the sun through the leaves. The grass smelled of ginkgo nuts, the nuts smelled of flowers, though the flowers did not smell. It was as though the storm had chased their scent away. Yasunari lay next to me, gazing up at the sky.

'Look, there, a hawk,' I said, pointing to the shape of the sky seen through the leaves. 'And over there, a giraffe.'

'That's not a giraffe. It looks more like you with your long hair.' His stomach rippled with laughter, and the sunlight peeping through the leaves tickled my eyes. 'I like watching the sky,' he said, 'it gives me a warm, deep feeling. I don't know exactly what—of belonging to something, or owning something, perhaps. I can carve any shape out of it. A bit of sky that is all my own.'

Ojiisan brought us discs of melon that he had cut. 'The sky can take any shape,' he said, 'because it is free. It has no limit. It can be anything you want it to be. If you feel a warm and deep feeling about the sky, it is because you have that warm and deep feeling within you. You can only feel this way if your mind is free.'

'Yes, my mind is free,' Yasunari replied.

'My mind is free, too,' I said. 'I feel a deep warm feeling inside.'

Ojiisan pared the flesh from the rind and gave it to us. We ate the fruit, juice dripping down our faces, which amused Ojiisan.

He was slim and stood perfectly erect. He had distinctive features: a chiseled jaw with a cleft, and high cheekbones. Thick eyebrows jutted above his clear, sharp eyes, and his striking silvery hair fell over his ears. He held up the leftover ring of fruit and asked, 'Yasu-chan, what is here?'

'Nothing.'

'There is nothing like nothing.'

'There was fruit there, but I ate it. Now, there is nothing except a hole.'

'Remember, nothing is the beginning of something.'

'Look, there is nothing in the middle, and I can see everything through it. I can see the sun. And when I move the ring around, the sky moves with it.'

'Don't see with just your eyes, see with your mind. Like in a dream with your eyes shut tight.' Ojiisan then told us a story, 'Once, when two monks were fighting—ne had said he saw the flag moving, the other that it was the wind moving—the Zen master said: "It is neither the flag nor the wind moving. It is your mind moving."'

Perhaps Yasunari understood what Ojiisan said; he was four years older than me. I tried to move my mind with my eyes closed, like in a dream.

Obaasan looked younger than her years. She was small, her skin was flawless, and her long hair was tied in a neat knot at the nape of her neck. When she smiled, her eyes wrinkled, and her eyebrows met in a delicate frown. She threw herself with absolute earnestness into all that she did around the house. She loved Yasunari, and he loved her back.

The morning sky diffused a serene and distant light, and Obaasan made us malted milk. I looked at the sky through the pockmarked glass of the malt bottle. I watched the light hop as I moved my head, or so I thought. In the evening, I watched the light again: it captured the colour of the sky, which was growing darker yet somehow clearer. It was just like the time Obaasan had pushed algae from the top of the pond, and I could see the orange-red carp in the green-blue water below. The sky was also an orange-red, dewy, glowing sheet of green-blue—my very own patch of coloured sky.

After dinner, we sat around the stone table in the back garden next to the pond. It was Ojiisan's favourite place. He had covered it with uneven stones that were now lined with a mist of evening dew. Here and there, neatly arranged around the cherry tree, was Ojiisan's collection of conch shells—reminiscences of the sea.

Later, Obaasan brought us cups of green tea and toasted ginkgo nuts. She lit a mosquito-repelling coil; its luminescence shone in the shadows. A bewildered sparrow flew from the roof to the cherry tree, a sudden summer breeze ruffling its leaves.

Obaasan sat in front of a large glass urn filled with water; it resembled a gleaming pearl in the moonlight. She retrieved a bottle of dye from a wooden chest beside her and poured it into the urn. Yasunari slowly began to pour different colour dyes one after another: white, red, blue, green, yellow, and then black. Obaasan swirled the water, and tendrils of colour seeped together, making it a muddy brown. 'Shibui,' she said under her breath.

'Shi-bu-i?' I repeated.

'Beautiful things are shibui; they are simple and subtle, difficult to define.' She stared at the urn as though meditating until the shadowy water stilled. 'The colours of life,' Obaasan said, clasping her hands together.

'It's dirty,' Yasunari laughed.

Ojiisan said quietly, 'You must find joy in simple things.' He lifted a large conch shell, held it in both his hands. 'Look at the shape of this shell. It has been formed by the sea passing through it. If you press it against your ear, you can still hear the water.'

Mosquitoes drifted in the darkness of the garden, circling my head. The reflection of the sunset in the pond was a shot of red-orange silk. Simple. Subtle. Indefinable. *Shibui*.

Beyond the pond, almost where the garden ended, not far from the Japanese maple tree, Obaasan had planted a cluster of azaleas. She trimmed the bushes regularly, and as she did, she talked to the flowers, which I thought was funny. Not far from the bushes, an anthill had sprouted from the earth. Obaasan pointed to a large red ant on top of the mound. 'The queen-ant,' she said. 'Listen, she's giving orders to the worker ants.'

Yasunari retorted, 'Silly Obaasan. Ants can't talk.'

Obaasan noticed a large spiderweb in the armpit of the maple tree. Several ants were trapped in it, all dead. She plucked the ants from it one by one, bits of the web still sticking to them. She dug a small pit, placed the ants into it, and then heaped the mud back over them. 'This is the ant-tomb,' she said, and plucked a weed from its roots and replanted it above the grave. 'Now the ants can talk to the plant through its roots.'

'But the ants are dead,' Yasunari insisted, 'and plants can't talk.'

'They have their own language,' Obaasan said. 'One day, we will go to the forest behind the cemetery. There, we will bathe in the forest—'

'—bathe?' I asked.

'Yes, bathe with all your senses. That's what shinrin-yoku really means,' Obaasan explained. 'You should look at everything around you, touch the earth and the trees, and smell the bark, the flowers; listen to the sound of the birds, the leaves rustling in the wind. And if you listen carefully, you can hear the trees talking.'

I asked, 'What do they talk about?'

Obaasan dusted her hands. 'The leaves are the eyes of the trees; they see all that happens around them and, deep in their roots, they collect stories: happy tales, sad ones, even scary ones. They have a good memory—forever and ever they remember. If you have a secret to tell, hug a tree and whisper into it. Its bark is full of ears.'

Obaasan's workshop was a black shed behind the cluster of azaleas. It had no door; only an indigo-dyed noren hung across its opening. Inside, on the shelves, arranged neatly, were bales of fabric. The room smelled pungent, like ink, and swatches of plain fabric were strewn on the floor.

'Shibori,' Yasunari said. 'You fold and tie the fabric and dye it.' He scrunched a square of fabric, tied it with a string, and dipped it into the vat of dye. He lifted it out—it was stained in rivers of indigo. 'Obaasan used to dye different kinds of noren,' he explained. 'But she stopped some time ago when Katayama-san stopped visiting. He used to help Obaasan—they had studied shibori together. He was a few years younger than her, and she liked him a lot, but Ojiisan didn't like him at all.'

Ojiisan called the loft his atelier; French for workshop or studio. The Japanese didn't have names for rooms, he'd told me. He wouldn't allow anybody to go up there, not even Obaasan; it was his private space. But he had stepped out of the house, and Obaasan had gone to the market, when Yasunari took me up there. 'It's got a glass roof,' he said, 'and we can see the sky.'

It was a large room that stretched across half the house. There were glass tiles on one side of the sloping roof, through which I could see the cherry tree and bits of the sky above. I closed my eyes and moved the sky-bits around in my mind, making patterns like I had with the kaleidoscope my uncle had given me. Arranged neatly on Ojiisan's low desk were a number of pencils, each meticulously sharpened. There was a wooden box that contained an assortment of items: tape, scissors, string, and cardboard frames of circles, squares, rectangles, and so on. Yasunari and I held each frame up and looked at the sky through them; they captured shapes of blue, each different, with tiny bits of clouds, the cherry tree, flowers, and birds.

On the shelves against the rear wall, Ojiisan's books gathered dust. It was pleasant, that smell of dust: comforting and old. Yasunari found a yellow folder with sketches of houses. He took the pair of scissors from Ojiisan's desk and carefully cut out their insides, so only the skeletal frames remained. We held the frames up towards the glass tiles and, all at once, slivers of sky occupied the houses. 'Look there, something is in the holes,' Yasunari said.

Under the shelves, in a trunk covered with a silk cloth, we found two photos of a woman, a locket, a hair clip, and some letters tied together with string. It was as Yasunari pulled at the string that Ojiisan walked through the door. His eyebrows stood on end, and his mouth turned down in a frown, then, with sad eyes, he looked at the leaves of paper strewn across the floor. 'These are drawings of the houses I have built,' he said, his voice almost a whimper. He picked up a sketch from the floor. It was of a woman, the same one as in the two photos in the trunk. She now had holes for eyes. When Ojiisan closed his, I shut mine and felt his sadness as well as my own. I clutched my mother's locket and I felt my brother's hand clutch mine. I felt calmed.

That night Ojiisan caught me crying. We had finished dinner, Yasunari had gone over to his friend's, and Obaasan was in the kitchen. I sat under the cherry tree. Alone, lonely, a flood of tears tumbled down my face. Ojiisan pulled me up by my arm. He didn't say a word but gently ushered me up the stairs to the loft. He sat down in front of the trunk and pulled me down beside him. 'Your uncle didn't want to tell you, but I think you should know. Don't tell him, though. He'll be upset.' He spoke softly. 'Your mother, your father, they both died in a fire.' He clasped my hands in his. 'You must have been about six. Your parents lived in a village not far from the Pakistan border. There was fighting, and houses and villages were burnt.'

'Why?'

'People do horrible things.'

'And my brother? I can't even remember his name. Did he die too?'

'Your brother? I don't know.'

'Where was I?'

'I don't really know.'

I closed my eyes. I remembered someone shouting, *Run, run, run*. I recalled running through the fields, but I couldn't remember anything else.

Ojiisan pulled away the silk cloth covering the trunk, carefully folded it, and placed it on the floor.

'This is my memory trunk,' he said. 'We have many memories, some happy, some not so much. But we can't move forward if our sad thoughts follow us. We must put them and anything connected to them in the memory trunk. That way, we can be happy some of the time. And, once in a while, we can open the trunk and revisit our sadness, but after, we must shut them away again.'

I took my mother's chain from around my neck and placed it in the trunk.

The next day, Ojiisan took Yasunari and me to see the house he was building. He carried a bag, in which he had packed, besides his pencils and sketchpad, a measuring tape, the cardboard frames, and a couple of coloured, textured bottles. The house was nearly complete. Ojiisan removed the cardboard frames from his bag and, peering through them, looked at the different parts of the house. He looked through the bottles, turning them slowly in his hands. He appeared satisfied with what he saw.

He explained how he built his houses. He made up his mind about the cooking space, the bathing area, and all the rest. He named them according to their size and not by what was going to happen in them. He set four wooden poles at each end of the house and decided where the doors would be fixed, and then he built the walls, leaving openings for windows. He then wrapped the entire house with a veranda.

'Why do all your houses have verandas?' Yasunari asked.

'They protect the house from the cold wind in winter, and in summer, they cool it.'

'How can the veranda do two things—keep the house both cool and warm?'

'In winter, the veranda insulates the house from the cold air outside. It's as if the house is wearing an overcoat. And in summer, the verandas, like a parasol, cast shadows that cool the warm breeze. The roof, like a hood, does this too.'

'I'll build a house without a roof.'

'How will you keep the sun out, Yasu-chan?'

'But the sun is nice.'

'It is too bright.'

'But light is nice Ojiisan—you can see things more clearly.'

'The house will become too hot.'

'The verandas will cool the house—you said so, Ojiisan.'

'And in winter, how will you sleep? You would feel so cold you'd want two quilts.'

'The verandas will keep me warm—you said so, Ojiisan.'

'And what will happen when it rains? Everything will get wet. Also, the birds will come in and make a mess, and Obaasan will get very angry.'

'Yes, Obaasan would get very angry.'

'So, we must build a roof.'

'Then I will build a glass roof, so I can see the sky and the birds and planes flying past, and then the birds and rain can't come in, and Obaasan won't be angry, and I will colour the glass so that it's not too bright inside and so the heat doesn't come in. It will be shibui.'

Ojiisan smiled. 'Nothing happens by whim, or even by chance. Everything fits into a predetermined plan. Do you know that each seed contains the idea of the tree? Just as each grain of sand holds the idea of the desert.'

I looked at the house and all its parts through the cardboard frames and bottles. The house was constructed using squares and rectangles, and I was looking at them through a circle and a triangle. I could see clearly where the door met the wall, where the roof met the sky, where wood met paper, mat, tile, and where they would all meet the rain. And when I looked through the bottles, I saw the parts of the house appear and disappear, separate, and reconnect. I could see more than I could see.

In the weeks I spent with Ojiisan and Obaasan, I learned new ways to think and see. They stretched everything. They stretched each day so it felt longer, they stretched their energy so they would never tire, they stretched belongings so they would last, and they stretched things so they could use them again and again. They even stretched their dreams whilst they slept, filling them with sunshine for the next day. They did not need much, and they made more from less.

Bangalore, 1993

My aunt's parents lived in Bangalore. I called them Tatha and Patti, although they were not really my grandparents. Tatha was slender, a bit frail, and had two dimples on one of his cheeks. His eyes were small, gentle. He didn't say much, though, when necessary, he muttered, *Decorum must be observed —dignity must be maintained*. He was a decorous man.

Patti came from a neighbouring village. Her parents were wealthy and they provided a large dowry. She was well trained in the art-and-craft of domesticity, and Tatha had agreed to wed her. She was uneducated and conservative, both in habit and mind, and was thirteen years younger than him. Tatha travelled all of the time and was too busy to be worried about any of this. He was, instead, occupied with the business of medicinal flowers, roots, and herbs.

Tatha's house was time-worn. The old wooden columns and doors collected and concealed, besides dust, stories and intrigue. The courtyard behind was lined with many rooms; some of them locked, their secrets hidden. The house had belonged to Tatha's father, who had had four children from two wives. Tatha's stepbrothers, stepsister, and their mother had all left home. Tatha had stayed. He was the eldest, the only child of the elder wife.

The house was already crowded when Patti came to live there. Attending to the needs and dictates of two mothers-in-law and their children took all of her energy and time. She was full of bitterness, and she was lonely; she had no time for friends, but she did have her daughter, my aunt. She smothered her with care and love when she was younger. Though later, she became overbearing, possessive. She unleashed her resentment of married life upon her daughter. My aunt tried to humour her; it was not through any deep affection but because Patti controlled her finances: five rupees for a treat, fifteen for a film, and so on. Patti was shrewd, a realist, my aunt was a dreamer who dwelled in fantasy. Patti laughed off these fluffs of fancy. Her laugh was wicked, as though she was planning something awful, this—and her excessive nature—terrified my aunt. She wanted to flee, and so she did.

After finishing college, she moved to Bombay. She had found a job with an NGO called Holding Hands, founded by her friend's sister, Sushila Srinivasan. Tatha was pleased, but Patti was furious. 'You should get married instead,' she said. 'You're not getting any younger. Look at your hair—it's already turning grey. And your face, with all that sun shining on it, has become dull and dark. Soon it will turn as black as soot and so dry you won't be able to tell the difference between your face and a buffalo's hide.'

This admonition, which lasted several days, unsettled my aunt. She washed her hair with hibiscus flowers and pomegranate rind, staining the grey strands a deep red. For days after, she pulled bits of petal and peel from her hair and stared a little longer in the mirror each day. She scrutinised her matted skin, the wrinkles that appeared between her brow when she frowned, and the disquiet in her eyes. The mirror's surface was misty but not because of dampness. She rubbed hard with her palm to remove the furrowed, yellowed patches, but they stubbornly remained. The mirror was old and fixed in a frame of pure Burma teak. It was part of Patti's dowry, and she had hung it with pride in the hall despite being cracked right down the middle.

'She's still young,' Tatha had argued with Patti, 'she doesn't need to get married yet.'

'But we have to start looking now,' Patti retorted. 'It takes a long time to find a good match.'

'Maybe she will find someone herself,' Tatha had replied, avoiding her gaze.

Patti's crinkled eyes grew large on her face. 'Over my dead body will she do such a thing. Mind you—I'm going to live very long,' she said, ending the debate.

'Go, face the world,' Tatha had said when it was time for my aunt to leave home. He had arranged for her to stay at a women's hostel. 'You'll make new friends.'

Patti called her frequently. She complained about the cook and the maidservant, her painful, swollen joints, and gave her news about boys: a fair one, a good one, a rich one, a wise one—either a friend's uncle's son or an uncle's friend's son. Somebody's son. Anybody's son.

My aunt told me it was through a senior colleague that she had met my uncle and added shyly that she liked him a lot. 'Let's get married,' she had told him within a year of meeting, and after a brief hesitation, he had said okay. Tatha was happy, but Patti had fiercely opposed their marriage. 'Grey-eyed men are deceitful, you must be wary of him,' she had warned at the wedding. 'He is too old and so very different from you.'

My aunt missed her father but hadn't gone to visit him since her wedding. She didn't want to face her mother's taunts anymore. However, Tatha was not keeping well; he was diabetic, and his blood pressure was high. My aunt took me with her to Bangalore. It was my third such trip: when I was six, I came to Bombay with my uncle, though I don't remember much of that; and two years later, he had taken me to Japan. It was, though, the first time I was travelling with my aunt. I was ten.

We stayed in what had been my aunt's room before she moved. My aunt told me it was just the way she had left it. The windowsill was lined with ceramic pots, plates, and bowls. In the corner was a large urn. 'I love earthen pots,' my aunt said. 'They remind me of the land. They were the sole consolation in my younger days. When I was sad, I hugged that big pot in the corner.'

Patti was not entirely pleased when I arrived that summer. 'You didn't have to drag this poor orphan all the way,' she told my aunt. 'What will she do here?' I could tell she didn't like me all that much. I wasn't one of her family, and she treated me as though I belonged to somebody else.

I dreamt of my mother that night. We played our favourite game: I pick out an object in the room—a bowl, a box of matchsticks, a potato, a spoon, a knife, or any odd thing—and she starts a story with it. She calls them story-seeds. When it is my turn, she says, 'Now, don't mess up the story. Use your mind's eye.' I look at her. She is nothing but a shadow, a faceless figure. I look for seeds to tell her story, but I find none.

I didn't sleep well and woke early the next day. I could hear Patti in the kitchen. I inhaled the warm, rich aroma of boiling milk and percolating coffee. The front door was open, so I stepped into the veranda and sat down on the steps. Already, every hint of night had faded. I mused over the morning light, which seemed to roll off the back of the clouds and ignite the water drops on the leaves. The wafer-thin air carried the echo of prayers and mantras broken only by the pneumatic honk of the milkman on his cycle, the moos of cows, or the barking of dogs. I heard the swish-swish of the broom on the compacted ground as the servant swept, then sprinkled water and drew a rice-flour diagram on it. Breakfast odours of soured rice-batter filled the air. The chanting had begun in the nearby temple, and prayer bells rang in every other house. Patti had finished talking to her Gods.

She awoke at the break of dawn, and after a cleansing bath, she dawdled up to the terrace and plucked jasmine flowers. It was her favourite flower. She had planted the vine when she had first come to the house. It was little then, no bigger than the size of her palm. It had since grown taller than Tatha's house. She watered the vine herself each morning. It had provided her deep solace in those early years when she had had to deal with her mothers-in-law. *So tiny and yet their scent is so strong*, Patti often commented. She found peculiar comfort in this fact: the insignificant too had might. She carried the white blossoms to the prayer room and offered them to the Gods lined within. She sang her prayers rather loudly, ringing the holy bell intermittently. The distant Gods would hear her, or so she thought.

Her Gods greeted and appeased for the day she filled water from the well in the backyard. She used the well water for cooking; she didn't trust the water from the tap. 'God only knows all who have touched it,' she said. As soon as the cook arrived, she sent him off to the market, and although she made breakfast for everyone else, she didn't eat it herself. She ate lunch before noon from a plantain leaf on the kitchen floor. She didn't like to be disturbed. Eating was a ritual for her. She looked down, absorbed with the food, whilst her eyes scrutinised the movements around her. No one bothered approaching her. In any case, there was something exceedingly acerbic about her during mealtimes. Even the crow—which had perched peacefully on the windowsill—was violently dismissed by a wave of her hand. She stuffed herself with the rice that arrived from her father's fields. Unlike Tatha, who insisted on eating with cutlery, Patti ate with her hand. She squashed the rice into the curry with her palm, shaped it into balls, and tossed them into her mouth. She chewed the food audibly, sounding like a wet grinding stone turned round and round on a still afternoon.

Tatha occasionally goaded her by saying, 'Eating by yourself will make you plump.' She replied to him with a loud grunt and an audible hiss through her nostrils; she didn't find him amusing. But he was not entirely wrong; she did admit she had grown rounder. She draped her stout body in silk sarees and wore gold necklaces and bangles and large diamonds in her ears and her nose, which shone brighter when she was vexed.

Patti did not remove her jewellery at night; they were a part of her just as her flesh, bones, and skin were; she slept with the weight of them. She worried about her jewellery and who would take them when she died. 'You be careful of the cook,' she told my aunt, 'he takes all the coconuts from the palm trees and sells them, then tells me, silly fellow, that they are male trees, that they don't grow coconuts. My jewellery is yours,' she repeated, 'be sure the cook doesn't take them.'

One morning Patti asked me to pluck some jasmines for her. Her knees were hurting, and she didn't want to climb the stairs. I took a basket of flowers to her in the prayer room, watched her offer them to all her Gods crowded in that tiny space. 'So many Gods here—' I said inadvertently.

'—then what,' Patti at once retorted. 'There are so many people with so many problems. They want so many things. How can one God alone deal with all of that? So we have special Gods for different things. And when there are bigger problems, our Gods will come down to resolve them.'

'The Gods will come to us?' I chuckled.

'Stop laughing like an ass. Yes, the Gods will come to us. People sin too much these days. They don't listen to the Gods or their elders. They tell lies and hurt people.' She turned to look at me. 'But if you are good, then you will go to heaven.' Patti pointed to the sky. 'Up there, above the clouds, far away, further than the stars, where the Gods live.' She closed her eyes. 'I will see all my Gods one day. But not yet.' She started ringing the bell, and in a loud, hoarse voice, she sang to them.

* * *

The maidservant Saroja arrived early each day with her daughter Malli, who was tall, terribly skinny, and a few years older than me. I was standing by the window when she came into the room, a broom in her hand. She stood there, the toes of one foot making awkward arcs on the floor. I looked up from her toes to a round face with startling eyes. Then, when I looked at her wide mouth, she smiled. The smile rushed to her eyes. 'Can I sweep here?'

I watched as she swept the floor. Her way of walking was arduous. Her body was sprightly, and yet she hobbled when she walked. She had a clubfoot, her long skirt veiling it from prying eyes. She didn't seem to care, though. 'It was this way when I was born,' she said with a shrug when I asked her about it. Her round moonlike eyes gleamed, 'I can't miss something I never had.'

She delivered newspapers in the morning before accompanying her mother to the house. Whilst Saroja went about her daily chores, Malli would carry out odd jobs her mother had asked her to do. One morning, I went with her to the terrace to collect the washing from the clothesline. We arranged them in two piles: Tatha and Patti's, my aunt's and mine—two families, neither truly mine. The parapet wall in front of us was broken, leaving a wide gap; below it was the sunshade over the kitchen window. Malli wobbled as she reached out and plucked the jasmine flowers.

'Don't pluck them,' I said. 'Patti will get angry. Jasmines are her favourite.'

Malli asked, 'Do you know why flowers are the most beautiful things in the world?'

'Because they are pretty,' I said.

'Yes, that, and they smell good, and they are soft to touch. Some even taste good. They also sing in the wind, but most of all, they make us happy. Aren't you happy when you see a flower?'

I had never considered this. Malli laid the flowers on the parapet wall and undid my plait. She gently pressed the flowers between her hands, and with care, rubbed them in my hair, as one would soap or oil. 'Now, your hair will smell good,' she said. 'You will be happy—all jasminey.'

Tatha appeared, and Malli hastily collected the clothes and limped back down the stairs. Tatha held my arm and walked me to the other side. He pointed to the trees—neem, banana, coconut, jackfruit, arinellikka, chikoo, guava, pomegranate, rain tree—and told me their botanical names, which were difficult to pronounce. He made me repeat after him: *Aza-dira-chta Indica*, *Musa Acu-minata*, *Psi-dium Gua-java*, *Punica Grana-tum*, and so on.

'This one is the tree of life,' he added, pointing to the moringa tree. 'Moringa oleifera from the Moringaceae family. It is nature's medicine cupboard. Every part of this tree is good for you.' He gathered the tiny leaves and put them in his basket. 'Patti will put these in the idlis,' he said. He plucked some more leaves, crushed them between his palms, and then gave them to me. 'Here, eat it.'

I chewed the leaves; they were bitter, so I spat them out.

'Bitter food keeps the belly happy,' he said. 'People who eat bitter food are actually sweeter.'

The gulmohar tree was in full bloom with radiant scarlet-orange blossoms. 'It is called Delonix regia and belongs to the Fabaceae family,' Tatha said, 'its flowers are good for pain in the bones.' He reached over the parapet and plucked a flower. 'Look, such madness in these colours, all the shades of fire. The French rightly called it the fleur de paradis.' He pointed out a single petal with yellow, white, and red markings. 'Botanically, this one is called upright standard petal. If you ask me, these coloured markings represent togetherness. When you grow with someone long enough, you end up alike. This petal grew close to the stamens, which infused their own colour within it. Emerson rightly said, "Earth laughs in flowers"—yes, it really does. Did you know each colour also has its own taste? Black and purple are bitter, pink and red are sweet, white and blue are salty, and sour is yellow or green.'

'Sour like a yellow lemon?'

'Taste has nothing to do with the colour of the flower, fruit, or vegetable. It's more complicated than that; you wouldn't understand. Come, let's go and give these moringa leaves to Patti. We don't want to upset her first thing in the morning—'

'—or she'll be black and purple,' I said, and Tatha laughed.

Later, as I ate the moringa idlis, I looked at Tatha and said, 'These are black and blue.'

'That's right.' He smiled.

Patti retorted, 'They are nice fluffy, white idlis. They are not black and blue!'

After breakfast, Tatha took me to his study. The shelves on the walls were lined with books, jars of dried root, leaves, and flower petals. He took down a small glass jar—that he had hidden behind the books—filled with little pyramids of brown palm-jaggery. 'I am not supposed to eat this, but you can have one,' Tatha said. 'Don't tell Patti, though.'

I bit into the pyramid. 'Pink and red?'

He stroked my head, 'My lovely granddaughter.'

Each passing day I faced unfamiliar circumstances, some of which perturbed me. I was forever breaking Patti's rules and being reprimanded for it. My aunt always shielded me, and Patti didn't like this. I could see it in her eyes—the manner in which her nostrils flared. Despite this, each day had promise. I felt unruffled when I was with Tatha, Malli, or alone. My sad thoughts, my troubled feelings, with a heartbeat of their own, were calmed. I was able to shut them away momentarily, in neat little drawers, deep inside me, and I was happy for a while. All jasminey.

Tatha, on the days he felt better, took me to the park, the library, or the plant nursery; my aunt took me to the fruit and vegetable shops. When I was not out with them, I was with Malli in the field next to the house. It was pleasant to sit on the grass, and whilst I pulled at it, Malli studied the clumps of weeds, how the sun had leaned on them, the effort with which the little bug crawled up a stem, and how the tiny yellow flowers absorbed the light, cast shadows that appeared to make the blossoms glide above the leaves. Or we were under the banyan tree on the street. Malli liked to draw. She sketched everything that she could see: flowers, trees, insects, cobwebs, people. She even sketched me. 'Keep it,' she said. 'So that you will think of me.'

One afternoon I took a sheet of paper from Malli's sketchbook and tore a circle in the middle. I asked, poking my finger through the hole, 'What is this?'

'Your finger.'

'No. What's around my finger?'

'My paper.'

'No…no.' I removed my finger and held up the paper. 'What's this, in the middle of the paper?'

'A crooked circle.'

'It's a hole, silly. Now, tell me, what's a hole?'

'It's the place where there is no paper.'

'No. No. You have to say *nothing*. A hole is nothing.'

'A hole is not nothing. It's something,' Malli said triumphantly. 'If you look up, the sky fills it, and if you look down, the grass fills it. A hole is something that can become anything you want it to. A hole is free.'

'Yes. A hole is shibui.'

'What?'

'Shibui. It's Japanese. It means something simple, subtle, and difficult to describe.'

'If it is difficult to describe, then why have a word for it?'

'I don't know. Ojiisan and Obaasan taught me this word.'

'Who?'

I told her about my trip to Kyoto, about Obaasan and Ojiisan, their pond with golden carps in it, and the candy-pink azaleas. 'Did you know flowers could talk?'

'Yes. They sing. They talk. They weep. And, if you crush them in your hand, you can feel the wetness of their tears.'

'And they laugh, Emerson said so.'

'Who?' And we laughed.

On another afternoon, as we sat under the banyan tree, I heard a shout, 'Malli! Ye Malli!'

'It's Meena-ma,' Malli said, pointing to the house opposite.

'Come here,' the old woman shouted. 'I have made hot potato bondas.'

'Come, let's go,' Malli pulled me up, and we darted across the street. Meena-ma was so tall that she stooped a little; she also had protruding teeth. Her silk saree, the colour of a paddy field, was mended here and there. Her house was small but had a veranda in front of the hall and an open courtyard behind it. A man sat on a long chair in the hall. He had on a white veshti, and his chest was bare. He plucked at the hairs on it, and every now and then, fiddled with the Brahmin sacred thread looped across his shoulder. He was small, diminished, and his round, hard belly seemed too big for him.

'Is that her father?' I whispered.

Malli said, 'No, that's her husband.'

Newspapers were stacked tall on the table next to him. Malli told me she delivered three newspapers to his house: *The Hindu*, the *Deccan Herald*, and *The Times of India*. Every time he spotted something that infuriated him, he would write a letter to the editor. They were mainly complaints about climate change, politicians' misdeeds, the growing greed and apathy of the youth, the increasing violence, and fraud. He cut out those letters that the editors cared to publish and pasted them in his scrapbook. Then he waited patiently for someone to pay heed to his grievances. He had been waiting a long time.

The hall was painted green, and the paint had curled away here and there. One of the walls housed pictures of the Gods and amidst them hung a bright calendar, the cheap, shiny sort that came free with large boxes of laundry soap. On it was a lurid picture of a starlet: her ample breasts suggestively covered with a sequinned magenta cloth, a dazzling green skirt wound enticingly around her hips. Her face was creamy white; her neck, arms, and the rest of her body, strawberry pink. Under the picture was a pile of square papers with the dates written on them; the first sheet said—in bold red—eight.

The old man stared up at the stationary ceiling fan—it was covered with soot and grease. The power had failed as it usually did in the middle of the afternoon. It was hot and muggy, and the old man fanned his face and neck with a folded newspaper. He yelled, 'That servant has not cleaned the fan again. Sha! If she keeps things so dirty, how can she have a clean mind?' He looked at the calendar. He rose suddenly and walked over to it, tore off several sheets until he came to the number twenty-eight. 'I have lost count of the days,' he muttered. He looked at the starlet, then at each of the Gods hanging beside her. The Gods and the starlet, both pink and smiling, seemed to keep each day safe for him.

Meena-ma took us into the courtyard and spread out a pai on the raised platform. She hurried into the kitchen and returned with two plates of potato bondas and coconut chutney.

'You live in the big house down the road, don't you?' Meena-ma asked me.

'Tatha lives there,' I replied. 'I live in Bombay.'

'When we lived in Madras, we had a big house just like your Tatha's,' she said.

'Then why did you come here?' Malli asked, her mouth full.

She pointed to the old man, 'He got a good job here.'

'Sha! What nonsense!' Her husband yelled from the hall. His voice rasping. 'You tell them it was because I am a Brahmin.' He beat his chest hard several times. 'We are superior, us Brahmins. We have brains.' He pulled at the Brahmin thread. 'This is the universe of knowledge.' He raised a fist in the air. 'Now the non-Brahmin government doesn't want us. They treat us Brahmins like pariahs, like dogs.' I could see the disgust in his eyes. He said, monosyllabically, 'Go. Go. Go. They shooed us out. First, the government was against anything British, then Muslim, and now Brahmin. This country has gone mad; the world has gone crazy. There are wars within countries, between countries, between religions, and between people of different faiths just because they think they are better. Look at what's happening in Kashmir. There were so many Kashmiri Brahmins there. Now it has been taken over by militants! No peace anywhere. I am tired now. I am so, so tired.' He rolled the newspaper tightly, swatted a fly, his anger directed towards killing the insect in one swat.

'Stop this ranting.' Meena-ma smacked her hand hard in her lap. 'They are just children. What do they know of these things, eh?' Her face was rough and wrinkled like crêpe paper. 'He was so miserable in Madras, ma,' she said. 'He worked so hard. He would have been the assistant general manager but was rejected because he was a Brahmin. So he left the job. I prayed each day to God. I broke so many coconuts at the temple, and God answered my prayers, and he got a good job in Bangalore. We needed money: my younger son had to be sent abroad for his Masters in Engineering; my daughter had to be married. So we had to sell our house in Madras and move into this tiny place.'

Her eyes shrunk into tiny holes. Her lips were flaked and dry. The diamonds on her nose and ears shone as she looked up. 'But my husband was not happy in his job here, he was not too well, so a year later he quit. After that, he has not worked at all. You need to be happy to be well, and you need to be well to be happy.' Her eyes were liquid with tears. She sighed heavily; her breath sounded loud in my ears. 'Krishnan, the kind man next door, arranged a loan for us from his bank. He sends us a basket of mangoes from his orchard each year. I gave tuition to his son, Mohan. That's how it started; I teach many children now. It keeps us going.' Meena-ma smelled of rose and sandal and it stuck to my skin for hours.

The old man let out a yell, 'That sparrow is pecking at the guava again. Wretched birds. Soon, there will be no fruit left. I am so tired of these birds.'

Meena-ma walked to the window and clapped. 'I'll tie a cloth on the fruit,' she replied. 'The guavas are ripening now —many birds will come.'

She wiped the sweat from her brow; sighed as she glanced at the old man. He had fallen asleep; his lower jaw had dropped, his mouth was agape, and a line of spit connected his lip to his chin.

Meena-ma packed some bondas in newspaper. She made two parcels, one for Malli, the other for me. On returning home, I gave the parcel to Tatha. 'For you,' I said and told him where I had got it. 'Meena-ma's nice,' I said. 'She sold her big house in Madras and lives in that tiny house down the street. She's a Brahmin; they have brains.'

Patti snatched the parcel from Tatha's hand. 'You got these from the tuition teacher's house, eh? Are you a beggar now? It's not as though I don't feed you enough. Stop eating in some stranger's home like an urchin. So what if she's a Brahmin and has brains; this whole street has only Brahmins, and we all have brains, okay.'

Tatha said, with a hesitant smile, 'What about that brick house where the Germans live?'

'The Germans are Aryan people,' Patti said with a sneer, 'they are German Brahmins.' She gave the parcel of bondas to Malli. 'Here, take it home.'

'Don't talk rubbish,' Tatha retorted. 'German's don't believe in caste and all that nonsense. Only fools do.'

'I am no fool.' Patti's face crumpled, and she suddenly looked very old. Malli had a Tamil word for this, though translated into English, it became a sentence: *Ripened before time*. Patti had ripened, and her eyes were now just tiny holes. If you looked into them, you felt as though you were looking into twin wells. Her lips were dry and chipped due to too much sorrow. At times like this, I even felt sorry for her.

Some days later, Patti took my aunt and me to Krishnan's house for his son Mohan's Poonal ceremony. Krishnan was a bank manager. He was wealthy and owned the mango orchard not too far away. He had invited all his customers, bank employees, and the entire street for the auspicious sacred thread ritual. When I asked Patti if Malli could come with us, she snapped, and her nostrils flared. 'Chi! She can't come—she's a non-Brahmin.'

Mohan was a few years older than me. He had on a white veshti, and his chest was bare. His mother and father were dressed in festive clothes, the priests chanted, and smoke rose from the sandalwood fire. As Mohan's head was shaved and concealed beneath a sheet of cotton, his father whispered the secret mantra in his ears and then looped the sacred thread across his chest. 'You have now entered Brahminhood,' his father declared. 'You will receive vast knowledge, and you must observe strict conduct.'

His mother fed him sweets. She said, 'I brought you into this world, dear son. You have crossed the threshold of innocence; you are grown now. You will follow in your father's footsteps.'

'So you are going to become a bank manager,' I asked Mohan later.

'I want to be a scientist,' he said.

I told Malli all about the ceremony. She grunted and said, 'Religion is nonsense. Rituals are silly. A thread around your chest doesn't make you special.'

'Mohan is special,' I said, 'he wants to be a scientist.'

'He's a clever boy,' Malli said. 'He collects the newspaper from me every morning. He reads the headlines out to me. He's my friend.'

'He's my friend too; I wrote down my address in Bombay for him.'

The next morning, when I woke, my aunt asked me, 'Do you have a new friend?'

I rubbed the sleep from my eyes. 'Yes, Mohan.'

My aunt shook her head. 'You were shouting in your sleep. *Tasneem, wait for me. Tasneem, don't go.*' My aunt looked worried. 'This is not the first time, either—who is she?'

'I don't know.' I left it at that. But for the rest of the day, it bothered me. Who was Tasneem? This hole in my memory felt like a dull ache: throbbing, persistent, and just when I had forgotten about it, it came back to me, as though through a rain-drenched pane, hazy, blurred.

I had woken early the next day and gone to the front gate with my toothbrush. In my mind, I saw a flash of Tasneem's face. She had long brown hair and light grey eyes. She stood on the other side of our gate, a toothbrush in her hand. I remembered her now; she was my childhood friend.

Gooru, the milkman, arrives ringing his bicycle bell. Tasneem and I rush out with our toothbrushes, foaming the toothpaste in our mouths as we ran, and—*1...2...3*—spat it out. Swinging on the old wooden gate, we sing the song: *Georgie Porgie pudding and pie, kissed the girls and made them cry*, that we had learnt at the missionary school. My mother yells, and I know then it is time to get ready for school. My mother stands by the door, waving her hand.

One afternoon Tasneem and I go to the market; my mother has packed some food for Rani-ma. Nobody knows who she is or where she came from. She has no home, and every morning she scrambles through the street whistling, cooing, hissing, and calling out to the dogs, cats, cows, rats. She listens to the creaking of ants in the crevices as they move across the walls. She sits by the temple, eating whatever food people have given her. A stray tear falls from her eye, and saddened, afraid, she rocks to and fro and sings out her usual refrain:

And who are alive?

And who are dead?

And who have gone?

And who are left?

Closer to the temple, Cheru, the cobbler, has an epileptic fit. People gather around him. Leather slippers, from well-walked feet, are placed around his body. Metal keys and coins are urged into his mouth. A sister from the missionary school circumscribes crosses in the air and across her chest, prays for poor Cheru. I start to cry, and Tasneem holds my hand. Rani-ma rushes to where we stand, shuffles us into the fields, and we scramble home.

Patti had given Saroja a bag of rice. 'Take it,' Patti said, 'it stinks. It's gone old.'

Saroja spread the rice on a mat in the backyard and plucked the stones and black lice from it. Malli sat beside her mother, not helping her in her task but instead making patterns with the grains. She had done the same but with broken tiles in her house.

She had taken me to the house one day; it was not too far. Just off the main road, a narrow alley ran down to the dumping grounds where migrant labourers had built their homes with materials salvaged from the dump: plastic bags, cardboard boxes, flattened tin cans, and so on. The air was awash with smells from the roadside market: the rotting vegetables, stinking fish, chicken feathers, and the whiff of roasted peanuts and piquant chilies. There was also the sounds of the people: bickering, haggling, shouting, voices sweet and harsh. Flies buzzed over sacks of brown jaggery, spiders climbed drainpipes, and vultures soared in the sky.

People crowded around the tea and snack stand beneath the peepal tree. The older women were plain, many of them unkempt. The younger girls were all brightly clothed, their faces made up: thick layers of face powder formed a sea-shore boundary beneath their chin. Scrawny men with bandits' moustaches in dark T-shirts, several sizes too small, sauntered along the road, flashy handkerchiefs tied around their necks.

I clutched Malli's hand. 'Don't be afraid,' she said, 'they are harmless, really. They like to dress up like the villains in Tamil movies—it makes them feel powerful, menacing even. Men are like that. They like to show off what they don't have. They are physically strong but weak inside, my mother always says.'

Further in, the lane widened and was surprisingly spotless. The huts on either side were the same: low mud walls with deep thatched roofs, beneath vigorous trees that grew tall. Motifs made with rice-flour adorned the entrances to each hut. Malli's house had a mosaic of broken tiles on the front wall. It had only one room and a small alcove for cooking. The floor and walls were patterned with pieces of tile pressed firmly into the mud.

'I did it,' Malli said proudly, 'I got the tiles from the dump.' She clasped her hands excitedly. 'I'm saving the money I get from delivering newspapers. When I'm older, I will build a house as big as Tatha's. And the floor and walls will be made of broken tiles. The courtyard will be full of flowering trees, and the moon will hang from the night sky. The rooms will all be open, without doors, so the scent of the flowers and the moon will seep into them. My children will run in and out all day.'

I laughed. 'How many children?'

'Only two, a boy and a girl, but definitely a girl. Though, I'd be happy with two girls. Girls are the best, my mother always says.'

On our way back, Malli stopped in front of a brick house; it belonged to the German couple. They were away, she told me. She talked to the watchman, and he let us in through the gate. Summer grass grew lush on the lawn, pockets of flower-beds carving through it. Malli plucked a few roses.

'Don't do that,' I said at once. 'They don't belong to us.'

'Ask the flowers,' she replied. 'Do they say they belong to someone? No, flowers belong to everyone.'

The pond under the rain tree mirrored the sky and the tree above. The reflection was beautiful: the edges of the clouds and the branches shone in gold and rust. The water was clear, radiating a serene glow. And, as I moved, the glow seemed to swallow my shadow. Malli lay beneath the rain tree, I curled beside her, and we looked up at the bright sky. 'Nobody owns anything,' Malli whispered to me. 'We belong to the world, and the world belongs to us. Everything in it belongs to us. Even if just for a short while.'

Her world was different from mine. Yet, at times like this, we came to inhabit a similar one, not unlike the upright petal and its stamens. At that moment, a cloud masked the sun and draped us in a shadow that made our world even smaller and a little more intimate. Yes, the world belonged to us at that moment.

Malli pulled her foot up and rubbed it.

'Does it hurt?' I asked.

She turned to me and said, 'Not as much as the hurt deep inside you. You look so lonely. Where are your mother and father? Did something happen to them? Is this why you are so sad?'

I was surprised; no one had asked me this before.

An indescribably gentle smile spread across Malli's face. 'You don't have to tell me. I'm not the kind who cares about this sort of thing. My father left when I was young. Life's like that.' She reached out and held my hand. There was something wild about her, and yet she could be so tender. I was unfamiliar with this kind of gentleness. I would continue to think of that moment for the remaining hours of the day. And also, briefly, into the next and the day after. Continuing to linger in some small corner of my mind.

I clutched her hand tightly. How could I explain the dismay I felt about not being able to remember my mother, my father, or my brother, or the intensity with which I missed them: they were the one thread that connected me to my own existence. That sadness consumed me, and a peculiar feeling churned inside.

The branches above rustled in the breeze, reminding me of a faraway willow tree that sighed in the distance.

We are in the garden, playing our favourite game, story-seed, my mother, brother, and me. I say, *Willow*, and my mother tells us a story:

'Many years ago, there was nothing on this earth but mud and water. Then tiny seeds rained from the sky and grew into a forest. The trees listened, watched, sang; the willows whispered in the wind. They were the caretakers of this new world. Then came the fish in the waters, insects, birds, and animals; they lived within the abiding rhythm of nature. People arrived last, and they misused everything around them; they cut the trees. The trees were unhappy, and the willows sighed. Sometimes, they bent down and wept.'

I felt my brother's hand in mine; it was cold and not as warm as I remembered. I felt as though I were touching an object that had misplaced its breath, quite unlike touching a breathing flower, a leaf, or the touch of the warm sky on my skin. Where had Arun gone? I shuddered. That was my brother's name, Arun.

I was living between two worlds: the one in my mind, temporarily fractured, and the one that lay before me. The rain tree was still; the breeze had abated, and the clouds above were bursting with a stagnant blaze. The stillness I found within freed me for now.

The next day Malli didn't come with her mother. 'The newspaper van turned up late,' she said when she arrived an hour later. 'Honestly, I don't understand why people care to read newspapers,' she remarked. 'Why do they need to know what's happening everywhere else? And in any case, most of the news is at least a day old. What's happened has already happened. Why bother if it doesn't directly affect us—it would be so wonderful to wake up and think, *I wonder what will happen today*, and not know until it does.'

Tatha, however, read the morning newspapers determinedly, page after page. He even read the horoscopes and the weather report, even though the climate didn't change much from day to day, only seasonally—as did life more or less. I wondered if he would agree with what Malli had said. As for me, I had no thoughts on it.

Later that morning, Malli picked up a cloth bag from the kitchen and took me to the mango orchard that belonged to Mohan's father. She scaled the gate with expertise, and I didn't try to stop her—it was of no use; Malli didn't believe in rules. Whenever I was with her, she coerced me into committing some small deed of mischief: harmless trespasses, innocent evils. Strangely enough, this little theft of mangoes made me cheerful, and we returned home with a bag full of them.

'Oh good, you picked mangoes,' Patti beamed. 'I hope that Krishnan didn't see you. He has a horrible temper.' She made a sweet-tart chutney with the mangoes, then filled a small bottle and gave it to Malli. 'Go, run, give this to Mohan.'

The next time we went to the mango orchard, I climbed the tree with Malli. I couldn't climb too high, but Malli deftly clambered to the top. When we returned from the orchard, Krishnan had followed us home. It was a Saturday, and the bank was closed in the afternoon. He complained to Tatha, his voice furious.

Patti screamed at him, 'What's wrong if they took some mangoes, eh?'

'Each mango counts,' said Krishnan. 'Money doesn't grow on trees.'

Patti retorted, 'You are too used to counting money in the bank—now you count mangoes on your trees, eh? By the way, your son Mohan eats the chutney I make with them with great relish.'

Tatha said softly, 'Be calm—dignity must be maintained.' He then asked Patti to return the remaining mangoes.

After Krishnan had left, Patti screamed at Tatha, 'Why did you have to give all the mangoes back. I would have made more chutney. You ate it happily enough earlier.'

Afterwards, Tatha took me to the market, and we returned with a bag full of mangoes for Patti.

I commented on our way back, 'It was such fun climbing the tree and plucking the mangoes.'

'I'm sure it was,' Tatha laughed, 'but, always remember, decorum must be observed.'

'Dignity must be maintained,' I replied, and he smiled.

The next afternoon Patti was napping when Malli noticed her keys on the kitchen shelf. Tatha had gone to a neighbour's house, my aunt was resting in the garden, Saroja was in the backyard, and the cook had gone to the market. We were alone. Malli picked up the keys, tiptoed across the passage, and I followed. One of the keys unlocked the door nearest the kitchen, which in turn opened into a smaller room that smelt dusty, smelt of faded memories. There was nothing in there except a bed, a mirror fixed to the wall, and a tiny stool. The wooden cupboard contained rows of sarees and books that smelt of mothballs.

Malli said, 'My mother told me this was Tatha's sister's room. She ran away from home. Soon after, her mother left with her two sons, one of whom died. It is rumoured he killed himself. He was young. Perhaps he was bored. His mother, it seems, was a stern and ambitious woman.' Then, in a brighter tone, she added, 'I will run away too. I want to go to the Himalayas. It is cold out there, and soft snow tumbles from the sky. There are no rules, no newspapers, and lots of flowers.'

Malli selected a pink saree from the cupboard and draped the silk around my waist. She pushed me onto the stool, undid my hair, and piled it on the top of my head. She pretended to blacken my eyes with kohl, brush my cheeks with rouge, and redden my lips with lipstick. With her finger, she stroked my lips to press the colour into their veins. 'Now smack your lips, like this,' she smacked hers. 'Ah, you look so pretty!'

It was then I heard a loud yell. I turned to see my aunt standing in the doorway. Malli hobbled past her. I would have, too, but at that moment, Patti came into the room and stared ferociously at me. I tried to stare back, but I was too fearful to look into her eyes. She swayed like a faulty pendulum, moving her weight from one foot to the other. A menacing quiver had started in her throat, her face convulsed, and then she screamed. I knew it was coming, that scream, like one can tell with a sneeze. It was coming for some time; her ominous silence had been twitching all along. Her eyes turned wide and red. The quiver in her throat had stopped, and a stream of frightful words thundered from her mouth, her voice tossing gusts of wind towards me; the air seemed to groan with each word. I wanted to shout back, but at that moment, my voice had mislaid the words to reply. And as I stood there, somewhat defiantly, she rushed towards me, yanked the saree off, pulled at my hair, and then gave me a hard slap on the cheek.

My aunt came to my defense. 'She's only a child.'

'Why are you defending her,' Patti screamed. 'It's not as if she's *your* daughter.'

I ran from the room and up the stairs to the terrace. Malli was there, staring absently at the gulmohar tree. The colour of the flowers appeared bleached in the brilliance of the light. I noticed a dragonfly on a branch slowly unfolding its wings. The distant buildings were shrouded by the sun-haze of early afternoon. I approached her, but she didn't speak. We stood so close that the smell of her floated before my nose. I was continually amazed at how easily she could dispel my gloom and fill me with instant delight. But now, she was at a loss, was immersed in a worrisome thought. I thought I heard a cicada whine, but soon I realised it was Malli who had made that strange, guttural sound. I could feel her tremble; then slowly but certainly, the quiver travelled through her body, and a long, murmuring giggle leapt from her throat. She clutched her belly with her arms and laughed uncontrollably. It took me only a moment, a little more than a second, and then I laughed out loud with her.

That night my aunt packed our bags.

* * *

Tatha died later that year, just as the rains had started. He was not ill. In fact, the last time my aunt had spoken to him, he had told her he was feeling better. But he had gone to bed one evening and not woken. My aunt didn't want me to go with her, but I insisted. I had liked Tatha a lot. Besides, I wanted to see Malli again—my obvious melancholy was tinged with a sliver of delight. As it happened, Patti requested that my uncle come as well—she needed a man to perform the funeral rites, so my uncle and aunt were compelled to bring me along with them. We took the morning flight and arrived just before noon.

We walked through the gate; I tried to peer through the front window, but the sun was shining on the glass, and so I couldn't see what lay behind. Patti was waiting by the door. She rushed to my uncle and said, hurriedly, 'The barber is here. You have to shave your head, bathe, and put on a white veshti—I have left it in the bedroom. Go quickly. Everyone is waiting for you.' My uncle refused. He told Patti he didn't believe in rituals; besides, he had already bathed. My uncle removed his shoes and walked into the hall. 'I told you he was a devious man,' I heard Patti tell my aunt.

The hall was crowded with people and smelled of boiled rice, the way Patti smelled all the time, and like her, it smelled somewhat rancid. Tatha lay on a makeshift bamboo stretcher, his head facing the door. It was the first time I had experienced the routines of death, and I didn't know what to expect. 'The head must face south,' my aunt whispered to me, 'in the direction where the Lord of Death, Yamraj, resides.' The Purohits had begun their ritual chants, which were every now and then, interposed by another Purohit blowing on a conch shell. 'In the old days, when there were no doctors, the bellow of the conch made sure that the person was truly dead,' my aunt explained.

I could feel everyone's eyes on me as I had my final meeting with Tatha. The flame from the oil lamp beside him was made pale by the intense sunlight pouring in through the window. His eyes were shut tight, and his nostrils and ears were stuffed with cotton. His face appeared calm, thoughtless. He most definitely couldn't see, hear, smell, or think, I thought, and at once chided myself. I held his hand and hoped he could feel the warmth on his now cold skin.

My aunt wept copiously, but Patti was tearless; perhaps her tears had dried, or she wept inwards, subliminally. She busied herself in the kitchen, making sweets and savouries for the neighbours and friends who dropped by to pay their respects.

My uncle covered Tatha's body with a white sheet, and people tossed flowers on his corpse. These flowers seemed so fresh against the starkness of the white cloth. I rushed up to the terrace, Malli close behind. We reached out and plucked the gulmohar flowers, returned with armfuls, and showered Tatha with them. After the ritual prayers were over, Tatha was ready to be escorted to his new home.

The women remained. Customarily, they were not permitted to enter the crematorium. Patti stood on the veranda to catch a final glimpse of Tatha. My aunt stroked her arm and said, 'You must cry your grief out, Amma. Cry Amma—you haven't cried at all.'

'People live to die,' Patti said matter-of-factly. 'It's a common destination for us all. Some are in a hurry—others are not.' She turned and walked back into the house. Her face was taut, dried-up, and set, not unlike a shrunken clay-head. Her ill-timed loss, the years of angst, were congealed deep inside. She simply couldn't weep. But I wept for Tatha, and my brother, Arun, wherever he had gone.

Patti hung Tatha's faded photograph beside the mirror, which had completely lost its shine—both old and dead to the world. Now she could complain to him as frequently as she wanted. 'I can still argue with him,' she told my aunt, 'and I am so glad that he can't say anything back.'

When my uncle left the next day, I hugged him tightly—my aunt and I had decided to stay a while longer.

'You can go too,' Patti said tersely. 'I'd rather be alone.'

A few days before we were to leave, Malli and I went across to Meena-ma's house. 'I saw her this morning,' Malli had told me. 'She's made rava halwa for us.'

Meena-ma's husband was resting in his chair, a newspaper

folded across his lap. The calendar read fourteen, although it was already the twenty-forth.

'Come, come,' Meena-ma said. 'Very-hot, very-hot.' She wiped her neck with the end of her saree.

The old man cast a glance at the window. 'Not a raincloud in sight. It's going to be a dry monsoon, I'm afraid.'

Meena-ma laughed. 'How can it be a dry monsoon? Monsoons are wet. And no need to be afraid—if we pray for rain, then it will come.'

'Sha! Rain doesn't come because of prayer,' the old man retorted. 'Nothing ever happens because of prayer—I have given up.'

'Don't say that. We always prayed in Palakkad. And it rained.'

'Pal-Kadd? Where's that?' Malli asked.

'In Kerala—I was born there. My parents had a big house, and surrounding it, green rice fields and tall coconut trees.' She placed her hands on her hips. 'Palakkad means *trees of milk*. Pala is milk,' she said, 'and Kad is trees—lots and lots of trees.' She spread her arms wide to indicate this. 'Almost a forest.'

Her husband chuckled. 'Pala-Kad. Then it should be *milk of trees*.'

'What? Milk of trees?' Meena-ma frowned.

The old man's eyes glinted with amusement. 'Well, in one way, the trees are made of milk; in the other, milk is made of trees.' He added, with a smile, 'One is *milky*, the other *treey*.'

'Rubbish,' Meena-ma said with a wave of her arm.

'What's *milky*? What's *treey*? It's simple,' she said, tapping her forehead with her forefinger. 'If you men ever worked in a kitchen, you would come to know. If you add hot water to rice, or rice to hot water, both ways, you will get piping hot boiled rice, no?'

The old man laughed. He looked happy. 'Well, actually,' he said knowingly, 'it is called Palakkad because of the pala trees. It is a forest of pala trees.'

Meena-ma frowned; her face crumpled like a leaf. 'Don't think you are clever—you don't know everything.' She turned to us, 'Come, girls.'

As before, we sat on the platform in the courtyard. Meena-ma brought us two bowls of hot rava halwa. I blew at mine to cool it down, but Malli ate hers hungrily. When she finished, she asked, 'I didn't see you for many days, Meena-ma. Did you go away somewhere?'

'We went to Madras last week to attend a wedding,' Meena-ma replied. 'Madras has changed so much. There are so many tall buildings now, many shops, so many cars, and flyovers. So many women go to work. In my time, after completing school or college, young women stayed at home until they got married. Now women want to make money. Young girls from good families star in silly films to make quick money.' Her eyes turned big and round. 'There are too many films now. In our time, there were very few and only religious ones. We would love to see the hero singing to Lord Krishna, to Lord Vishnu, and then watch the Gods sing back. Now villains are heroes.'

She removed her glasses and rubbed the sweat that had collected on the top of her nose. 'But, you know what the biggest change is? People believe even more now. All this belief in God is to do with jobs. In the end, I think,' she clenched her hands below her chin, 'everything has to do with jobs. The riots, crime, violence, are all because of jobs.' She sighed; it came out as an elongated hiss. 'My son from the US had come down for the wedding. He wants us to go to Chicago. He has a big house. My husband is very happy and wants to go. Maybe he will get a good job there, too. By God's grace, I may get a job in a school there as well.'

'So, you are leaving?' Malli asked.

'I am thinking we should go. There's nothing much left for us here. Only this morning, I went to the nearby temple to offer a coconut. I pray to so many Gods that I think they all know me by name.'

'If you go, what about your Gods?' Malli asked.

'Our Gods will go with us, of course.'

I looked out of the window. Outside, the guavas were wrapped in red muslin. A koyal sat on the branch of the guava tree. *Coo-coo-coo*, it cooed.

Afterwards, we walked to the German couple's house. As always, they were out. We lay under the rain tree, looking up at the leaves. They were closed. I remembered something that Tatha had explained: 'The leaves fold up before the rain, that's why it is called the rain tree. The leaves also close at sunset, and in Malay, it is called Pukul Lima, which means five o'clock.' Its pink flowers resembled tiny powder puffs, and they dropped down on us in the breeze.

Malli picked one up, twirled it between her fingers, its silken threads dancing. She said, 'Nothing should last very long. When it does, it stops being beautiful. We should be like flowers—we should fade away.'

'My parents were too young to die,' I told her. 'They hadn't lived that long.' The rays of the sun peeping through the branches made me oddly happy, even if it was a sad day.

The wind rustled through the branches, and its closed leaflets tumbled down upon us. The wind howled, and the branches of the plants surrounding the pond brushed against each other. The sky had turned a purple-grey; the clouds thick and black resembling fists with veins of light pulsing through them. A gentle rain fell on us. Malli turned on her side and put an arm around me. 'I'll miss you—' she said, '—don't fade away.' Her face was wet.

Bombay, 1994

My aunt went to Bangalore more frequently now and stayed longer each time she did. I didn't go with her—I couldn't miss school. She gave me news about Patti and Malli on her return. Patti had employed Malli full-time—she slept on the floor in Tatha's sister's room—and she still took raw mangoes from the orchard, which Patti made into sweet-tart chutney. Patti had bought Malli schoolbooks, and she was also learning to read and write. The pain in Patti's knees had worsened, and she couldn't walk without help. Malli supported her as she staggered around the house—which I thought was odd as Malli herself ambled clumsily. 'She is a good girl,' Patti said.

Whenever my aunt left, I always sent small gifts with her for Malli: sketchbooks, colouring pencils, paint, fancy hair clips, and so on. Malli would send me a sketch or two, and dried flowers that had been pressed between the pages of a book. But of late, she hadn't sent me any of those things. When I asked my aunt, she said, 'Malli is grown up now. She wears sarees, has other interests. She disappears from the house in the evening. Patti gets very angry.'

'Where does she go?'

'I don't know. Her mother is worried, though. She wants her to get married; she has found a boy for her. His father is the watchman of that brick house down the lane.'

'I know him,' I said.

'You know the boy?'

'No, his father.'

'Malli doesn't want to get married to him. She's quarrelling with her mother all the time. But Saroja is adamant. She's making arrangements for the wedding. Patti has given her many silk sarees that belonged to Tatha's sister. One day Malli disappeared in the afternoon, and when she returned, Saroja locked her in the room for the rest of the day. Patti unlocked the door after Saroja had left and gave Malli some food.'

'Did Malli cry?'

'Not that girl. She never cries. She behaves as though she owns the world.'

'You remember the tuition teacher and her old husband?' my aunt asked me when she returned. 'They were planning to move to Chicago. They had their passports, their visas, even their plane tickets. Well, the old man was staring at the fan, complaining about how filthy it was, when all of a sudden he couldn't breathe. He gasped several times, then fell back on his chair and died.' My aunt paused, 'The son flew back from the US; he will take his mother back with him. Poor woman.'

Patti was filled with a sudden fear after the old man had died. 'That's the third death on this lane. The Lord of Death is waiting at the corner of the road—I see his shadowy figure at night, walking up and down,' she told my aunt. 'He has got his eyes fixed on me; he particularly likes people who live alone, but I won't let him take me—I'm not ready yet. I may have lost some teeth and hair, but the rest of me is still intact.'

The last time my aunt was there, she had asked Patti to move to Bombay. 'Never!' Patti had retorted, 'I will not live under the same roof as that grey-eyed man. My corpse will leave only from this house.'

'She has lost the use of her legs but not her tongue,' my aunt told me.

A few days later, Patti called my aunt. She said Malli had run away from home and had taken all her things with her.

When my aunt told me this, I said, 'I think she has gone to the Himalayas.'

My aunt rushed to Bangalore and stayed there all month. Patti's brother was there too; he had decided, much against Patti's wishes, to take her home with him. 'You can hardly walk,' he told her.

'I will depart only from this house. My legs will last, as will the rest of me, until then. I won't need my legs when I'm a corpse,' Patti argued. Her brother, however, was unwavering. My aunt helped her pack. Patti took with her four sets of clothes, the silver utensils, all the pictures of her Gods, a silver lamp, and the holy bell. She even tried to uproot the jasmine vine at the back, but couldn't, so she let it be. She gave all her jewellery to my aunt. 'What will I do with all these,' she said, 'it's a village out there.' My aunt refused, and Patti said, 'They are pure 24-carat gold and blue jaguar diamonds, and the rubies are straight from Burma. Give them to your daughter.' She gave my aunt Tatha's photo and the cracked mirror from the hall. 'I am moving on,' she said, 'I don't need any reminders.'

My aunt put Tatha's house up for sale. The wooden columns and doors that had collected dust over time liberated their stockpile of stories and intrigues. Buyers were reluctant, superstitious. They had heard about the sister running away from home, about the brother killing himself. *The house is cursed*, they said. By the time my aunt sold the house, I was already in college.

I went with my aunt to Bangalore to bid farewell to Tatha's house. The jasmine vine at the back had wilted along with all the bushes and shrubs. The gulmohar tree, however, was in full bloom, so I plucked an upright petal and pressed it into a book. As if on cue, Patti died a few days later. We were still in Bangalore, so we arranged for a taxi to take us to the village; it took us half the day to get there. Lush fields and fruit orchards surrounded us. We turned off the main road and into the village. Small houses—with neat front gardens—were scattered here and there; in them grew palm trees, papaya, guava, banana, and pomegranate trees. A dusty road led to a big house. A jasmine vine crept over the front wall, which bloomed profusely in clusters of delicate flowers. Its scent was everywhere. The funeral rites had already begun when we arrived. Soon it would be time to bid Patti goodbye. In the photograph of her in the hall, she wore a withered look that seemed to say farewell. As she had said, she didn't need her legs for this final walk.

My aunt didn't shed a single tear as they took Patti away; she was silent and resolute, and because of this, I didn't know how to console her. She stood in the doorway to catch a final glimpse of her mother. I said, mirroring what she'd said to Patti at Tatha's funeral, 'You must cry your grief out, Amma. Cry Amma—you haven't cried at all.'

'People live to die. Some are in a hurry—others are not. Patti took too long to go.' We stood watching Patti's body until we could see her no more. My aunt took Patti's photograph down from the wall. 'I am taking her with me,' she told her uncle. 'I can talk to her, and she won't answer back.'

After the cremation rites were over, Patti's brother returned home with an urn of her ashes. 'What do you want to do with these?' he asked my aunt. She dug the earth from around the jasmine vine and buried Patti's ashes deep under the ground. 'She loved jasmine flowers,' she said. 'Now, she'll sleep well.'

On our return to Bombay, my aunt hung Tatha and Patti's photographs on either side of the cracked mirror in her room. That way, they would remind her of all that was.

* * *

Mohan was in Los Angeles studying computer sciences and wrote to me regularly, to which I replied with all the news. I once reminded him of his wish to become a scientist. *A computer scientist earns more money*, he wrote back. His father had told him so, he said. I was disappointed, but I didn't tell him that.

I had enrolled in a three-year course in journalism at Bombay University, and Yasunari had finished his architectural education and was now employed by a leading design firm in Kyoto. He regularly sent me pictures of the buildings he was working on. Ojiisan and Obaasan sent me cards as well. They didn't write anything in them as I couldn't read much Japanese. They chose each card carefully, however, to suggest the seasons, their mood, their colours. The envelopes, also, had been diligently selected, as were the stamps, not based on their price, but their content. I looked forward to their mail as well as S-san's letters and parcels that continued to arrive at the beginning of each month.

At a creative writing workshop I attended, I was given an assignment. We were asked to spot an interesting character in a public place and to follow them. We were told to imagine what they did, who they were, who they lived with, and so on, and write about it. My fellow students found the task ludicrous, but I found it rather intriguing. I turned it into a habit of sorts. Whenever I felt alone or glum, I followed someone from the bus stop or market all the way to their destination. It became an amusing pastime and was good for my legs. I had a separate diary in which I recorded these secret expeditions.

My aunt took me to her NGO. It was her last day; the arthritic pain in her joints was troubling her, and she could no longer work full-time. We waited in the small office to meet Sushila, the founder of Holding Hands. Time had a different count here, tiredness a different shape, and patience extended languidly like a long yawn. On the wall were posters asking for contributions of rice, lentils, baby food, and for volunteers. *Even a day of your time will help*, it said on one of them. After some time waiting, a worker led us to another room. Sushila came out of the bathroom; her face and hair were damp. She wiped her face with the end of her saree. 'I was here all night,' she said, 'a baby had been abandoned in a dustbin.'

My aunt spoke to her and then left to meet her co-workers. Sushila ordered tea. She was from Bangalore, she told me, but was educated in Bombay. She studied sociology and law. 'This centre is now twenty-four years old, and your aunt has worked here for seventeen of those. Let me tell you how it started. One day, you see, a baby of eleven months was abandoned in a cinema house. It was a night screening. A taxi-driver brought the baby to me. I didn't know what else to do, so I took her to the hospital—the baby was not well. Fifteen days later, I took her to an orphanage, but they said they wouldn't take her.'

Her voice was shrill and seemed to come from the depths of her stomach. 'So I decided to keep the child. Soon I found more abandoned children who needed somewhere to live. I went door-to-door for food and money. Over the years, I have picked up babies from dustbins, railway compartment toilets, manholes, and from my own doorstep.' She sniffed and wiped her eyes.

She gave me an anguished glance. 'One day, I got a call from a policeman. A young girl was disturbed and had given birth to a child on the street—that was five days before they called me. By the time I found her, the baby had died. Rukmini is with the centre now.' Sushila gazed at the hoarding outside her window: an idyllic picture of a beautiful village with smiling children beneath a brilliant sky. *Be a proud Indian*, the advertisement read. She looked tired, exhausted. Her voice broke, 'How can I be proud?'

A tall, skinny girl walked into the room. 'This is Rukmini,' Sushila said, looking up at her. A young child accompanied her; she must have been six or seven with round eyes as large as planets—deep within them a perpetual startle. I could understand this; I had felt that way when I first went to live with my uncle and aunt.

The girl ran to Sushila and said, 'Please can I have toffee. Please.' Sushila opened a drawer and gave them one each.

'What's your name?' I asked the little girl, who was now chewing her toffee.

'Sheela. No, Geeta. Umm, Radha.'

'You're such a sweet girl,' I said, stroking her hair.

Sushila said, 'Her name is Maya. She has been to three orphanages already. Each called her by a different name, so she's confused. She ran away from the last shelter; we found her on the road with a pair of street dogs.'

Maya asked, 'Please, can I have another. Please.'

Sushila gave her one more. 'Last one, okay.'

Maya turned to me. 'This is for you—you are sweet.' She pressed the toffee into my hand.

After the girls had left, I turned to Sushila and said, 'I have no classes on Thursdays, can I volunteer?'

My aunt and I walked through the little alleys of the slum, retracing our steps to the main road. There were piles of broken stones, dust rising from them, filling the air. The huts were built with salvaged material and jute cloth, appliquéd several times over with the hardship of living below it. Crows and rats scavenged through heaps of garbage, and snot-nosed children ran about, stray dogs racing behind them. 'I built the centre in the slum,' Sushila had said, 'land was cheap, but more so, because it's a constant reminder of the sufferings of the migrants who are forced to move to the city, their miseries of living a life on the edge, endlessly.'

Much of Sushila's gloom had rubbed off on me. The alleys we had walked through mirrored all that she had described. Closer to home, the surroundings appeared familiar, assuring, like the glowing, advertised India; it wrapped itself stickily around my shoulders.

At home, a brown envelope had come for me. I checked the address on the back; it read *Himlyas*. Inside were several sketches, dried flowers, and a note scribbled on ruled paper:

i am happy

i am well

i have hassband

i have 2 chilran – 1 and 3

i am neer himlyas – not faar – can see it

many flowers here

shi bu yi

It was during the second year of college that the nightmares began. They came suddenly, and I was unprepared and afraid. They had a predictable pattern: there was always fire, and as the fire grew fiercer, I ran. I heard screams and cries and then people and events collided in bizarre episodes, unreal and incomprehensible. I woke up sweating, panting as though I had run for miles.

I felt weak for days after as though I was recuperating from a strange illness. There were no visible signs, no high temperature, rashes, bleary eyes, or any such symptom—which I would have been glad about had they occurred; at least then, I could have taken refuge without having to explain or be awkward.

'Are you not well?' my aunt asked.

'You look pale,' my uncle said.

'Why are you not eating?'

'You're so thin. You will disappear—'

One night I felt something deep inside like a tight knot of feelings. It felt weighty, raw, and too real to be just a dream. Perhaps it was a memory.

In it, I can hear Arun shouting, *Run, run, run*, and then I'm running through the fields towards my house. Pyramids of fire rise high into the sky. Thick black smoke curls into darkened clouds and spreads over the hills. I see people rushing from their homes carrying small bundles of luggage: utensils, clothes, photographs. Many houses are burning. People crowd on the road: men, women, children, old and young; such terrified people. Some of the men are shouting, and the children and women are crying. One woman laughs. It is madness: the shouting, the crying, the shrill laughter. I run up the hill to my house. It is engulfed in flames. I cry out: *Ma. Papa*. They aren't there. They aren't anywhere. I hear my name. My uncle approaches me and takes me in his arms. He cries on my shoulder, and I weep into his chest. 'Thank God, you are alright. Where's Arun?' My uncle shakes me by my shoulders. 'Where's Arun?'

I lay exhausted from the dream. My throat parched, my body covered in sweat. I went to the kitchen for a glass of water and found my aunt squatting on the floor, weeping inconsolably. She slapped her head with her hands and cried, 'My child, oh my child.' I sat down beside her and wrapped my arms around her shaking body. She rested her head on my shoulder. I stroked her hair, then bent down and kissed her damp cheek. It was not the first time that I had found her crying in the kitchen, but it was the first time I had consoled her. She often burst into tears suddenly, and without warning, her tears flowed relentlessly. I could never understand what prompted them. My uncle seemed to know, and though he cared, he disregarded her despair. He was a firm believer in letting things be.

I heard my aunt complain to the family doctor about my situation when he visited to check my uncle's blood pressure.

'She keeps getting headaches. She doesn't sleep enough.'

'It's a part of growing up,' the doctor replied. 'Why don't you have her eyes checked? Maybe she needs glasses.'

My aunt took me to an optician who told her there was nothing wrong with my eyesight. She took me to a dietitian next, then a gynaecologist, then a neurologist, and when nothing they prescribed worked, she concluded that I must, instead, be suffering from a mysterious ailment that was incurable through modern medicine: a curse or possibly the result of karma. She made the obligatory rounds of the various temples, making offerings that differed according to the weight and reach of their powers. She insisted that I accompany her and face the Gods myself, that I offer my own prayers to them. But her Gods didn't seem to heed us, so my aunt took me to a god-man next. 'He knows the language of the Gods,' she said.

Concerned, her friend introduced her to a clairvoyant who drew up two charts of numbers, one for her, the other for me. Reading her chart, he proclaimed that her health would improve in the coming years, that she would live happily to be a very old woman, and that she would be lucky enough to witness the marriages of her grandchildren. This pleased her a lot.

She was, however, dismayed when she heard what he had to say about my future. 'She will marry someone from a foreign land, but he will bring her misfortune.' And as for my headaches, he was unable to predict anything of substance or offer any assurances.

So my aunt woke each morning at five, bathed and washed her hair. She wore her silk sarees—a different one each day, smelling of mothballs and starch—and with a lamp set on a plate, she circled the desert rose and prayed to the dead, imploring them to bestow peace and health upon me. The drops of water that dripped from her hair made concentric circles on the floor—a tantric mandala. She recited the mantra the clairvoyant had given her in a shrill voice that startled the sparrows in the trees. The old man next door switched on the light in his room and peered out from his window. With a deep breath, he filled his lungs with the dew-air of dawn.

Each day after her tryst with the sacred plant, my aunt scrutinised me carefully to find any indication of change, but there was none. The desert rose did, however, grow healthier and sprouted new leaves with all the additional attention she bestowed upon it. The sparrows learned to sleep through her morning rituals, and the elderly gentleman now slept with his window closed. I despaired.

It was time for the Navaratri festival, and this cheered me up. It's a popular festival in Bombay and celebrated over nine nights, beginning with the first moon phase after the dark moon. My aunt was a vegetarian, and though my uncle cooked meat every now and then, my aunt had separate utensils for this. During Navaratri, she observed a strict fast and diet. She cooked spice-less vegetarian meals with seasonal vegetables, legumes, and pulses, and without onions, garlic, cereals, or grains. Neither eggs, meat, nor alcohol were consumed during these nine days. The night before Navaratri, my aunt went up to the terrace to offer prayers to the absent moon. On the evening of the next day, my aunt wore a silk saree, and I a silk kurta over a long skirt, and we joined the people gathered in the street to offer prayers to the Garbo, a clay pot symbolic of the womb of the universe. Amidst pulsating drums and folk songs, we danced, clapping our hands to the rhythm and moving in concentric circles. Often we struck sticks called dandiyas as we moved. We danced in the memory of the battle between the Goddesses and the Demon King late into the night. On the ninth day, the half-moon beamed down upon us; I looked up and saw a flock of birds fly across it.

I developed a high fever that night, and it did not subside for many days, and when it did—after overdosing on medication—my hair began to fall out. Within a month, I was partially bald. My aunt consulted several doctors who prescribed light and heat therapies, vitamin-reinforced creams, and zinc-laced hair tonics. One of them tied a cloth dipped in hot sesame oil on my head. Another made tiny incisions on my scalp, squeezed lemon juice in the cuts, and then covered them with a paste of tea leaves, fish oil, and seaweed. 'Don't cover her scalp,' another said, 'let the skin breathe.' But my aunt, who could not bear the sight of my bald head, bought me scarves in different colours and implored me to wear them at all times. At night, when I examined my head—which was now covered with cuts and burns—I could smell a fish-weed sea.

My aunt took me to a psychologist who said the cause was most likely childhood trauma. 'There are huge gaps in her memory,' he said. 'They involuntarily resurface as dreams, nightmares. Her memory will surely return in due course, bit by bit. In the meanwhile, I suggest she gets absorbed in a hobby, some form of sport, music, or dance.'

My aunt enrolled me in a Bharatanatyam dance class. I went each day after college, six days a week, and was so exhausted that I slept a deep, sound sleep every night. My aunt was most happy when she noticed shoots of new hair on my scalp. It didn't take too long for my hair to grow back, and I put on some weight with the rich diet I was now eating.

I was nineteen when I took part in the group dance—the Dashavatara—a series of stories about the evolution of mankind told through the avatars of Lord Vishnu: who periodically assumed incarnations to set right an erring world. In his final avatar of Kalki, he initiates a new beginning from all that remains of the world.

I had heard these stories before; someone had told them to me when I was a child. Her skin was the colour of peeled cinnamon, her nose delightfully upturned, and her eyes were translucent like flower petals in the rain. She had a gentle voice, almost a whisper.

'Matsya, the fish, was the first avatar,' she tells me. 'When the world floods, Manu chooses a pair from every species, loads them on a boat, which a horned fish then pulls all the way to the Himalayas. Then, with her face raised to the air, in a voice that rings through space and walls, she sings the story.' Her eyes are shut, and her face is laced with rose and gold. With her other hand, she caresses the air, massaging it, curling it up and up and out of the window.

On the evening of the dance concert, my aunt dressed me in my costume. Behind the wings, my teacher arranged the folds of my saree and secured the flowers in my hair. 'Yours is the most important part,' she said, 'you are the Sutra Dhār, the narrator. You observe the world, you listen and tell the story.' A tinge of anxiety touched her eyes, and then I was on stage. I heard the sound of sticks, drums, and cymbals, the rhythmic sounds which guided my feet, hands, and eyes into ecstatic dance movements: I became a fish, a wild boar, the snake Vasuki. Churned Mount Meru in the ocean. I became a tortoise, turned half-man, half-lion. I became the dwarf, Vamana. I assumed the avatar of Rama, Parasarama, Krishna, and the Buddha. I liquefied into mammoth waves, flooded the earth. Flames leapt from my eyes, scorched the universe.

That night I dreamt of fire with a sucking-swallowing mouth—the fire-mouth sucked me into its flames—armpit-sweat—pulse-ablaze—I danced—the bells broke from my ankles—cut my feet—I bled—blood mixed with the flames—became redder—Arun screamed—*Run, run, run*—the heat of the fire was still in my eyes—I covered my ears with my hands—I ran.

In the summer of that year, I completed my course in journalism. I took a part-time job at a newspaper called *News First*, a name that was nothing as lofty as the *The Times of India*, or the *Herald*, *Express*, and *Telegraph*, all of which sounded important, dignified. I worked at the office three times a week, and the remaining three days, I volunteered at Helping Hands. The assignments I did for the newspaper were uninteresting.

The editor asked me to write fillers to occupy the inches of paper, and what I wrote was inconsequential. He made me write fake letters to the editor, so—remembering the letters Meena-ma's husband had written—I penned missives about climate change, politicians' misdeeds, the growing greed and apathy of the youth, increasing violence, and fraud. I was bored and unhappy. Besides, the impoverished children at Helping Hands, and particularly the plight of Rukmini and Maya, saddened me. My aunt was concerned for me. When my uncle was preparing to leave for Tokyo, she pleaded, 'You must take her with you—a change will do her good.'

* * *

We were at the airport hours before our flight; many passengers had likewise arrived early. There had been a terrorist attack in Kashmir, and the country was on high alert. The counter hadn't opened yet, and so I pushed our luggage trolley towards the waiting area. We sat down next to a middle-aged man who was reading a newspaper. He was dressed in a bright red T-shirt and a navy-blue jacket. He had meticulously covered his bald spot by combing long, fine strands of hair from one side to the other.

He surveyed my uncle from the corner of his eye. 'London?' he asked.

'Tokyo,' my uncle replied.

'Ah, Tokyo, very expensive.' He made a clucking sound with his tongue. 'Myself, Jasu Shah. JS for short. From

Ahmedabad. And you?' My uncle didn't have time to reply before JS continued, 'I'm going to London to meet my son. Married. Two children. A doctor. Works in a hospital there. Has a big house in Islington.' He plucked a photograph from his wallet and thrust it in my uncle's face. 'My grandchildren. Two years, girl. Five years, boy.' He showed him another photograph. 'My son.' He shook his head. 'Now he has a beard. I tell him not to keep it—mistaken for being Muslim.'

I saw an elderly man walk towards us. He wore a white kurta and pyjama, and over it, a tight, short, black coat that was too small for him. His long beard had traces of henna in it. He carried a large aluminum trunk covered with a floral cloth stitched to fit. Slung over his shoulder was a small cloth bag.

JS placed his hand on the seat next to him. 'Occupied,' he said tersely.

The old man limped past him and sat down on the vacant seat next to me. Something fell out of his bag, a small jar of Vaseline. I picked it up and handed it back to him. His lips were chapped. 'Shukriya, beti,' he said. He looked around anxiously. He glanced at his watch and then turned to me. 'Will you look after my trunk? I want to go,' he pointed to the toilet.

'No,' JS retorted. 'You take your trunk with you. We can't look after it.'

The old man looked at him and frowned. He turned to me. 'Beti, is he with you?'

I pulled his trunk closer to me, 'It's okay—you go.'

The old man hastened towards the toilet.

JS grimaced. 'It's dangerous to look after other people's things. He is a Muslim; you can't trust them. He may have hidden something in his trunk. What if he doesn't return?' He picked up his luggage and moved away.

The old man returned shortly after, thanked me, collected his trunk, and hurried towards the counter. We followed him across to the security aisle. There was a long queue, and we stood not too far behind the old man; behind me was JS. The security officials were thorough; they asked the travellers to take off their jackets, to empty their pockets, and they checked their shoes at random.

The officer inspected the contents of the old man's cloth bag. He picked out the jar of Vaseline and dropped it into a bin, watching the old man as he leafed through his passport; he then ordered him to remove his shoes.

'Why?' the old man asked.

'It's routine,' the officer barked.

'But you didn't ask the man in front or the man in front of him. Why me?'

The officer frowned, his lips curled. He shook his head in exasperation. 'Take your shoes off now and put them on the belt, here.'

The old man stiffened. Hesitantly, he took his shoes off and placed them on the belt; he wasn't wearing any socks. His voice broke as he said, 'I know why you are checking me —it is because I am Muslim.'

'See, I told you,' JS breathed into my ear. 'Nobody trusts Muslims.'

A fragment of memory returned to me. I could hear someone utter the very same words: *Nobody trusts Muslims*.

I wake to sounds of shouting and wailing in the middle of the night. Out of the window, I see our neighbours being pulled from their homes, hands behind their backs. Tasneem is howling. Not too far away, I can see a line of people being marched down the main road.

'Where are they taking them?' my mother asks my father.

'To Pakistan road.'

'Where is Pakistan road?'

'Far away.'

'Why?'

'Because they're Muslims, they're not allowed to live here anymore.'

'They have lived here for as long as I remember—why can't they live here now?'

'Because nobody trusts Muslims these days.'

All I could recollect were my parent's voices. I tried to remember my mother's face; were her eyes as grey as mine? I tried to remember my father; was he tall and gentle? I couldn't remember my brother at all.

Kyoto, 2002

Obaasan had grown frail, and she now stooped a little. Ojiisan hadn't changed much aside from the accumulation of fat around his stomach and a benign growth on his neck. He had named it Tora—*Tiger*. The doctor had suggested removing the lump, but Ojiisan had declined. 'Tora is a part of me,' he had said firmly to Obaasan, 'and it will live with me.' Yasunari was now tall and wiry, and his crop of black hair drooped around his face. His eyes dazzled when he smiled.

It was in an advertisement on the television that Yasunari had seen it. It was a week after I had arrived in Kyoto. 'I am going to buy that,' he declared.

Ojiisan grunted, thrusting wet noodles into his mouth. 'Where are you going to put it?'

'You can fix it to the old wooden bathtub, and it comes with a solar panel which you can put on the roof,' Yasunari explained.

'Don't touch that roof,' Ojiisan said. 'I had it repaired only last year. And don't touch that tub either.' He paused, thinking it over, 'You mean you're going to fix that hideous gadget to it? I made that tub myself, out of the best pinewood. Its skin is still smooth after all these years. Ah! But what do you know of such things.'

'Have you felt the slime inside the tub, Ojiisan? I think you should throw it out. We should get a new fiberglass tub. Why do you like to keep old things?'

Ojiisan's face turned red, his wrinkled hand clenched into a fist. 'You will never understand the value of old things,' he said. His attachment could not be attributed simply to a lack of money or even close-fistedness. It was, for him, a way of living.

'Don't be upset, Ojiisan,' Obaasan cajoled him. 'Times change. People change. Things change. We must also change. My mother always threw out her old things before every New Year. They become tsukumogami—they bring sadness and misfortune. Sometimes even death.'

I memorised the word tsukumogami; it was the first time I had heard it. I would ask Obaasan about it later, I thought. It was not a good time to interrupt.

'Here, Ojiisan, have some spaghetti.' Obaasan spooned the pasta into a bowl, topped it with roast chicken, and grated cheese, and added a few drops of olive oil. 'Yasunari wanted me to make it,' she said with a smile.

Ojiisan pushed the bowl away. 'I won't eat this stuff.'

'Ojiisan, why don't you try a little,' Obaasan implored. 'It's just like our soba.'

'Are there any leftovers from yesterday?'

'Don't be so stuck in your old ways, Ojiisan,' Yasunari said.

'I may be old, but I am not stuck in any way.'

'There isn't any leftover food,' Obaasan said. 'Where are you going?' she called out as Ojiisan started to leave.

'I am going to the ramen shop around the corner.'

'Suit yourself.' Obaasan's face, although grim, cloaked a chuckle.

I felt sorry for Ojiisan. 'I will go with you,' I said.

After a hot bowl of ramen, on our way back home, I asked Ojiisan what tsukumogami was.

Ojiisan snorted loudly. 'It's a spirit that resides in old objects. They trouble and trick people, so people discard old things from the house—clothing, kitchenware, furniture—before each New Year to ward off calamities caused by these tsukumogami. This old custom was called susuharai or house cleaning. Obaasan practiced it every year when we were first married. It's a stupid superstitious ritual. I put a stop to that rubbish, she doesn't do it anymore.'

A week later, Yasunari installed the solar heater which provided—at a considerably lesser cost—a tubful of piping hot water. Ojiisan refused to bathe in it. Instead, each evening after dinner, he strolled to the public bath, towel, soap, and scrub cloth in hand, a look of defiance on his face. However, the subsequent week he came down with a cold and was therefore compelled to use the bathtub.

'It's only because of this cold,' he said, emerging out of the misty bathroom. 'The water doesn't smell fresh.'

Obaasan gave him a large bowl of hot miso soup to cure his cold and resentment. 'You must admit, the water is hotter now,' she said gently, her lips curling into a hesitant smile. Ojiisan defied her with his silence.

His resentment persisted as we walked down the street the next day to buy fish for the evening meal. The clouds broke as we strolled down the slope, and a soft, watery sunlight fell over the pavement. 'That one,' Ojiisan pointed to an old wooden house with a large garden. 'I built that, and that one across the street. See how beautiful they are.' Unconcealed joy shone on his face. We passed a modern building. 'There used to be a lovely wooden house here. It had green tiles on the roof and in the garden, a beautiful persimmon tree. Look at this hideous box of glass and concrete. These young architects sell their outrageous ideas to unsuspecting people who should know better. People must learn to respect and preserve old things.'

We passed a swarm of women outside Toscana—the new Italian restaurant. They were middle-aged but dressed in trendy Parisian clothes. They were noisy—I heard snatches of French and English in their conversation. 'Yasunari's mother dresses like those women,' Ojiisan muttered. 'She has cut her hair short and coloured it like a persimmon. She had long black hair when she married Shigeru. Red hair suits her, though, she is rather fiery. Yasunari told me recently that she bought a red sports car. Must match her hair.' He clicked his tongue in disapproval.

'You don't like her much,' I said.

'She doesn't like me,' he replied, 'and that's why they moved to Tokyo. After her holiday in Italy, she cooks Italian food all the time. Italian noodles are not like Soba or Udon. Their noodles come in different shapes and sizes, and they are drenched in sauces and smothered in cheese. I never eat cheese; it's nothing like tofu.'

Not far from Toscana was À La Mode, a chic hair salon. Ojiisan peered through the tall glass front. The salon was like a bunch of cherry blossoms—all pinks and creams, the mirrors gilded with gold leaf. The hairdressers were in uniform—a silken pink blouse and a short vermillion skirt. It was busy: women under hood dryers, women with their hair in rollers, young things with perms in the roots of their mane. Blond. Burgundy. Chestnut. Heads of hair cut, snipped, straightened, curled, coloured, and blow-dried. And the music was so loud it permeated through the glass.

The owner saw us and stepped out of the door. She was also middle-aged, her face painstakingly made up, and her short vermillion hair was streaked with cobalt blue. She greeted Ojiisan, then turned to me, fingered my hair, 'So silky and soft. You should wear it short; it will frame your face.' She made a shape with her hands. 'And russet will suit you very well. I can give you an appointment for tomorrow.'

'Excuse me,' Ojiisan said, averting his eyes, and walked hurriedly past her without another word. I followed him. He stopped in front of the public bath he had recently frequented. He waved a dismissive hand at it. 'I wonder how long this one will last.'

We stopped at a red light, and an elderly man bowed to Ojiisan and walked on. Ojiisan said, 'He was a master builder like me, though, he doesn't build anymore. He wanted his son to help him, but his son became a dentist, moved to Tokyo, where he lives alone in a flat in one of those tall concrete buildings. I haven't seen him in many years. Neither has his father, who lives alone, poor man; he lost his wife a few years ago. He has a beautiful old house. There's just him and his house, and they endure, all that is left, together.'

We crossed the street to the fish shop. The fishmonger greeted Ojiisan cheerfully. Ojiisan peered into the tub containing prawns and lobsters and decided to buy whelks instead. The fishmonger dug the meat out with a knife, diced it on a wooden board, and returned it to the shells. He wrapped them in paper.

'I hope you are not going to shut down your shop,' Ojiisan said with a grimace.

'I am what I am because of you.' The fishmonger bowed and said, 'Take care—it's getting cooler. Don't catch a cold.'

Obaasan set the bowl of tsubugai no nitsuke on the table. It was Ojiisan's favourite dish—whelks and bamboo shoots simmered in saké. Accompanying this dish were prawns sautéed with negi and slivers of ginger, furikake (a dry topping for rice made from a mix of dried vegetables, egg, nori, and bonito flakes), tiny bundles of steamed spinach topped with toasted sesame seeds, silken tofu in soy sauce, and pickled vegetables. Obaasan spooned hot rice from the cooker into bowls for us.

'You have made a feast, Obaasan,' Ojiisan remarked. 'Itadakimasu.'

'I wonder why Yasunari is so late,' Obaasan said.

'He must be out getting drunk with Hiroo. He spends a lot of time with him, I have noticed.'

Obaasan looked pensive. 'Yasunari's going away this weekend to Kamakura; he will come tonight. Leave a couple of whelks for him—you know how much he likes them.'

Ojiisan said to me, 'Why don't you go with him to Kamakura? You should visit Hokokuji Temple. You can see the stunning moso bamboo grove and the tea house where you can enjoy a bowl of matcha.'

'He's going for work,' Obaasan said. 'I don't know if he will take her.'

'Of course he will,' Ojiisan retorted. 'I will tell him.'

'Thank you,' I said. I wanted to go to Kamakura. I wanted to be with Yasunari; I missed him. Besides, my uncle would be in Tokyo at the end of the month, and I would be returning to Bombay with him.

Just then, I heard the sound of the front door slide open. 'I am home,' Yasunari called out.

Obaasan's face lit up as he walked into the room. 'Yasu-chan, you are just in time,' she said.

'Sorry, Obaasan,' he muttered. 'I returned to leave my stuff at home and change my shirt. I'm meeting Hiroo for a drink. I will be having dinner with him.'

'I want to talk to you,' Ojiisan's tone was fairly serious.

Yasunari didn't seem to notice the sternness in Ojiisan's

voice. 'I'm late.' With a wave of a hand, he rushed out of the room. I smelled the whiff of cologne, and then I heard the front door slide shut.

Ojiisan skinned two peaches, cut them into wedges, and placed them on the plate in front of me. Despondently, I plucked a whole peach from the fruit bowl, skinned it with my fingers, and bit into the fruit. Ojiisan laughed. I remembered eating mangoes this way, juice dripping down our fingers, my brother's and mine.

'Let's sit in the garden,' Ojiisan said. He picked up his sketchpad and pencil from the side table and walked out of the rear door.

'You go,' Obaasan said to me. 'I will clear the table. Be careful,' she added, 'there are many mosquitoes.'

I joined Ojiisan in the garden. He flicked through the pages of his sketchpad until he came to a page with an unfinished drawing. 'This is the new house I am building; maybe the last. A friend wants a house with a traditional exterior, but his wife wants a modern interior to fit in all her new gadgets. She wants a living room *and* a separate dining room.'

Obaasan brought us tea. She sat down beside me, said, 'Mariko-san has a living room and dining room separated by an inner courtyard, which has a juniper tree next to a pond. It is as though the outside has come inside. It's so nice. And a part of the roof over the dining room is made of glass. The house is so bright and not at all dim like these old houses. The long kitchen overlooks the back garden; it is also bright.

And her house doesn't have a veranda. "It makes the inside dark," she told me.'

'Rubbish!' Ojiisan snorted. 'A veranda is most important. How can you have a house without an engawa?'

Obaasan retorted, 'You don't like Mariko, and so you don't like her new house!' A smile rose to her cheeks.

Ojiisan stared at his sketch petulantly. Finally, he spoke, almost a whisper, '*Dodes'ka-den*. It's a film by Akira Kurosawa about Roku-chan, a slum urchin who pretends to be a tram driver, and he calls out to passengers, *dodes'ka-den*, *dodes'ka-den*, mimicking the sound the tram makes. This young tramp and his poor father, who live in a shell of a car, fantasise about their ideal house with large windows. The film didn't do very well.'

Obaasan added, 'But the message was clear: times are changing.'

Ojiisan sighed in resignation. He tore out the page from the sketchpad and crumpled it. 'I would rather be dead than change.'

A sudden breeze sent the loose pages of Ojiisan's sketchpad flying. I scuttled across and retrieved them, gave them to Ojiisan one by one. The last one was the sketch of the woman with holes for eyes. Obaasan looked at it, shaking her head. Ojiisan, surprisingly sensitive to her glance, took the paper from me. It slipped, caught the drift, swirled, coiled, and rose high beyond the tree. Ojiisan looked up at it. 'I can hear music —' he said and added almost to himself '—that moment, when the paper dips and soars, snatches my breath away. I feel it in my heart.'

Obaasan's face remained impassive as he uttered this, and all she said was, 'So many mosquitoes.' She plugged in the mosquito repellent device, slipped a blue tablet into its face, sat down, and looked up at the moon. Besides its light, the only glow came from the electronic gadget. Ojiisan started sketching again. Obaasan frowned, 'You will spoil your eyes —it's too dark.'

He looked at the rough sketch he had made, paying no attention to the expression on his wife's face, then his eyes lit up. Turning to me, he said, 'In the old days when carpenters built houses, they used an umbrella to cast shadows on the site. It helped them position the house close to the shadows so that it was dim inside and not too bright, like Mariko's house.'

'Stop, Ojiisan—that's enough, okay,' Obaasan's lips curled. Her face was glowing with the rush of cold air. She scuttled indoors and returned with a brown furoshiki wrapped around her head. She held out a pink one with cherry blossoms on it. 'Wear it, or you will catch a cold,' she told me.

Ojiisan took the scarf from her and spread it on the stone table. 'Ma, a room, is like this furoshiki. This cloth can be used to cover the head, but it can be used for wrapping and carrying things as well. A traditional Japanese house, like a furoshiki, wraps and parcels space. Wrapping is an art form. The veranda—engawa—wraps the house. En means a bond, a relationship, an affinity. The engawa is a connection between the inside and the outside.' Ojiisan cleared his throat, looked sideways at Obaasan. 'A ma has no definite boundary, and so the rooms flow into each other without any separate function. There is no living room or dining room, only ma.'

Obaasan was quick to retort, 'With so many things in this house, your ma has nowhere to flow!'

Ojiisan's lips settled into a grim smile. There was a momentary hush, and the cool breeze caressed the leaves. A sparrow flew from the roof to the cherry tree. 'Ah, the sound of the solitary bird flying in a sukiya,' Ojiisan said. 'When you go to Hokokuji, you will see that the sukiya—the teahouse—is just like the old Japanese house. In the mizuya, the tea utensils are washed, people wait in the machiai, and roji, the garden, is the rite of passage. It is the first point of meditation. The three elements in the roji—the stepping-stones, water basin, and stone lantern—all symbolise willingness. The stones reveal their willingness to be stepped on, and the water basin, its willingness to be pure. The stone lantern denotes the willingness to be free of things.' He smiled. 'It's important to be willing—'

'—of course, Ojiisan, everything is as you will it,' Obaasan intervened.

Ojiisan ignored her comment; he took up the explanation again, 'When you go to Hokokuji, you will notice two large boulders in front of the sukiya. Perfection is impossible to achieve, so one has to resort to imperfect ways. Let me explain: there is the sukiya, beautiful in itself, and then there is the roji, equally beautiful. How can we ever make a perfect connection between the two? It is better to leave each as they are and have something imperfect, something impermanent to connect them, like the stones. The sukiya, and every little thing within, illustrate the impermanence of things. Inside, you will notice the emptiness. It is not about the things left out but more so the absence of things. When the ceremony begins, you will observe that each gesture is deliberate and delicate. Every move is fragmented, left to you to piece together. You may well be unnerved by the gaps between the movements and moments.'

Obaasan laughed. 'Ojiisan, stop all this serious talk. Look at the full moon, isn't it beautiful.' The moonlight seemed lovelier than ever through the branches, and its reflection in the pond was breathtaking. A bird darted across, and a yellow leaf, broken from a low branch, glided into the pond; it floated on the water's surface, a stain on the mirrored moon's face. I reached out and grabbed the leaf making the moon whole again.

Ojiisan smiled. 'Sorry, I talked for too long,' he said, 'but let me add one last thing. When you are in the sukiya, you must strip yourself of all but the simplest and the plainest self. Only then will you be a true partaker of the ritual. You will see a scroll hanging in the alcove, and flowers arranged in the tray below. These will elevate your sense of sight and smell. The sound of water boiling in the iron pot, the water dripping from the bamboo pipe, the sound of a solitary bird flying, the rustling of the kimono, a distant temple bell—all will enhance your sense of sound. The tea itself is very bitter, and the sweet cake is very sweet. They will heighten your sense of taste—from bitter to sweet. When you hold the bowl in your hands, your sense of touch will also be roused. So remember, when you go there, keep your eyes closed and your senses wide open.'

Obaasan shouted with childish excitement, 'Look, you can see the shadow on the moon's face. It is supposed to be an image of a rabbit pounding mochi with a mallet.'

A smile flickered over Ojiisan's lips. 'Obaasan, you sound like a girl. It is merely a play on the word mochizuki—the autumn, full moon—which also sounds like the word for pounding mochi, mochitsuki.'

That night, as Ojiisan, Obaasan, and I stared at the moon, the intense scent of the tablet drove the mosquitoes away.

Kamakura, 2002

'Make a wish,' Yasunari said, 'and paint one pupil in black.' We were at a street shop outside Hokokuji Temple that sold a variety of mementoes and keepsakes. Yasunari bought me a red papier-mâché Daruma. It had a painted face, but the eyes were white, without pupils. 'When your wish comes true, paint the other pupil black.'

Yasunari strutted steadily on with an air of confidence and the knowledge of being amidst all that was familiar, as for me, I swayed backwards and forwards balancing on the geta—the Japanese clogs that Yasunari had bought me—adjusting to a new way of being. Yasunari held my hand as I wobbled through the moso bamboo grove. The sukiya was in an incredibly beautiful garden, and flat stones of varying shapes led to it in a meandering sort of way. The plinth of the sukiya was a little more than a foot above the ground. Two flat boulders placed before the plinth posed as steps to ascend—a mute suggestion of the virtue of imperfection.

The interior of the sukiya was austere, faded, with an absence of colour. A pale scroll hung in the alcove, and below it, a tray of arranged flowers. The tea ceremony lasted over an hour. As Ojiisan had warned, the stillness was initially unsettling; the only sound was of water dripping, boiling, the brush in the bowl, the tinkling of bamboos outside, a distant bell, and the flutter of a sparrow. Equally unsettling was Yasunari's impatience: the ceremony failed to interest him, and he fidgeted the whole time.

The teishu, an elderly man in a black yukata, served the tea and sweet cake with a humility unknown to me. I drank the thick and dark brew slowly, it was bitter, and the sweet cake was unimaginably sweet.

Yasunari leant close to me and whispered, 'Imagine if this teahouse had been a glass box. We could have seen the vast garden outside, and the expanse of the sky above. It would have been stunning.'

I closed my eyes, felt Yasunari's hand cover mine. A sparrow fluttered in my heart.

Early the next morning, Yasunari took me to his construction site. The building was nearly complete; essentially, it was a glass cube with a large concrete dome, fitted with glass discs, and held up by red, claw-shaped steel ribs. The glass cube was set in a postmodern concrete frame that incorporated classical arches, gargoyles, and columns—a surreal show of the old and new.

'My take on Christopher Wren's dome,' Yasunari said excitedly. 'He was an English astronomer, mathematician, and physicist, and later became a famous architect. He designed the renowned St Paul's Cathedral in London.'

Ojiisan's houses, and everything within them, was part of a sustained tradition. There was comfort in the fact that they were real, predictable, and therefore reassuring. Yasunari's creation, however, seemed to me to be a product of his hallucinations. The more closely I tried to know him, the less I did.

Yasunari was busy for the rest of the day, and the morning of the day after. I was on my own, so I bought an inexpensive digital camera, and with it, I roamed the narrow streets. There were houses with little gardens in which shrubs blossomed in the right places, and the trees grew to the right height, flowered in the right colours. The birds in the trees sang a honeyed tune. Everything in the winding streets of Kamakura complied with an unseen artistic blueprint.

I took the train to Kita-Kamakura the next day and walked to the Kenchō–Ji temple, the oldest Zen monastery. Strolling up the garden path, I looked out for the affinities between inanimate things: stones, sand, water, fountains, lanterns, juniper trees. My camera couldn't capture their connections; however, it could capture the peonies of many different colours, and the white and pink roses. High up on the garden path, I stopped beside a bizarre sculpture of a bird-man with wings and a long, beak-like, pointed nose.

'Tengu.' I heard someone say softly. I turned to face a monk. 'Tengu is the Japanese bird demon,' he said. I was surprised; he spoke English rather well. 'He is the guardian of the mountains and forests. However, Tengu is considered an enemy of the Buddhist faith; he leads monks astray with his devious tricks.'

Obaasan had told me about Tengu and Oni. Now and then, she would throw roasted soya seeds out of the door, shouting: *Oni wa soto! Fuku wa uchi!*—ogres outside, good luck inside. Oni was an ugly, fierce ogre. He had wild hair, sharp claws, and horns. His skin was red, or blue, and he wore a tigerskin loincloth. He brought disaster, disease, and bad luck into the house. Tengu was a trickster. Each time Obaasan couldn't locate something, she would say: *Ah, that Tengu is at it again. He has hidden it somewhere.*

'Come with me,' the monk said. I followed him to the Hojo hall. We discarded our footwear on the steps and entered the meditation room. Several monks and visitors sat on cushions arranged in rows on tatami mats. The monk asked me to sit down beside him. I sat cross-legged, left foot over right thigh. My hands in my lap, right hand over left, thumbs lightly touching. I straightened my back and pulled in my chin. My eyes, like his, were open, looking slightly downwards.

'We will do zazen meditation now,' the monk said. 'Breathe in and then breathe out very slowly. Count your breaths. Empty your mind of thoughts and feelings. Don't be attached or involved with anything.'

I noticed the thread that had come loose in the tatami's stitching. I averted my eye, tried to empty my mind, but instead, I thought of Obaasan and Ojiisan. They were almost one person, living each other's differences together. Ojiisan resisted change: he mostly wore a yukata and ate only Japanese food. Obaasan, unlike him, adapted to new things judiciously: she wore trousers as they were convenient, and she depended on modern household gadgets for the same reason. When Ojiisan was not around, she even enjoyed pasta, pizza, and lemon cake. Unlike them, my uncle and aunt were two separate people staying together, their joys unshared.

Next, I tried to think of my brother. I remembered the birthmark on his face, a bluish-red patch, which spread from his chin to his neck, in the shape of a small country. Recalling this minute aspect of him sent a shiver down my spine. I held my breath and counted. I had reached eight when a shout went off in my head—*Run, run, run*—and all of a sudden, I found clarity in an incident that had been nibbling away all along, one I couldn't remember clearly, until then. Now it surged through my entire body and became a dull ache in my chest.

It is a Saturday. The market day. A day when farmers from many villages assemble to sell their produce. Villagers arrive in small trucks from near and far to stock up on goods for the week. My uncle is with us; he arrived the night before from Bombay. My mother asks Arun and me to get her some things from the market.

The morning sun has hardened, crisping the air. Arun and I walk down the hill to the market. Suddenly a group of men run into the street screaming, their eyes fierce. They set a shop on fire, then the next one, and then an explosion rips through the air. Arun clutches my hand, and in a voice gone shrill with fear, he screams, 'Run.' The birthmark on his face reddens, and I can't move. 'Run, run, run,' he shouts. I run but let go of his hand, can see him running up the street without me. I shout out, but he doesn't hear me.

I ran from the Hojo hall to the back of the temple. I sat on a bench near the pond and caught my breath. After a while, the monk joined me, and we sat in silence. The colours reflected in the water caught the light, melded, and turned luminous. There was something untainted about the monk that made me confide in him. I told him my parents had died in a fire; I told him my brother was missing. There was nothing more to tell.

I detected a slight American accent as he spoke. He told me he was born in a concentration camp. His grandparents had moved to California in search of a better life. But in 1942—after the attack on Pearl Harbor—all Japanese Americans were rounded up and sent to these camps. 'Life was difficult there,' he said. After the war ended, his grandparents and parents moved to a trailer park in Los Angeles. Eventually, after many relocations, they moved to Berkeley, where he studied landscape architecture. His interest in Zen gardens brought him back to Japan, where he studied the gardens in Kyoto, Nara, and Kamakura. He had come to this monastery and hadn't wanted to leave.

A momentary ache, as vast as an abyss, united us. When the moment had passed, the monk said, 'In the Ryōan-ji garden in Kyoto, there are fifteen stones arranged in the sand in such a way that you cannot see all the stones at once. The Daisen-in garden, created by a monk, is fifteen yards in length and only three yards wide. You can't see the whole of it; you can only see it as you move. It is the Zen way—to move, to go with the flow, because in the end, there will be nothing but a void, after which there will be a new beginning.'

His eyes were wide now, not grave, as I would have expected; instead, they contained something of the innocence that comes with age and endurance. He looked straight ahead and uttered to no one in particular, not even himself, 'The war, the struggle, the suffering was undesirable but inevitable; we must move on.'

He closed his eyes and sat still, unmoving. His hands placed on his lap were withered and thin, and remarkably long lashes sheltered his wrinkle-set eyes. It was my first encounter with a monk, as close to God as I had been. My uncle was not pious, and neither was I.

'Are you an atheist?' I had once asked my uncle.

'Not exactly,' he replied, 'there's a difference between *not having* and *losing* faith.'

I took pictures of the moss-lined stone islands in the pond, the stunted trees, the undulating grassy bank, and the woman in a blue kimono.

'May I see?' the monk asked. I gave him the camera. 'I like the way you compose your pictures,' he said, looking at the one with the woman in a kimono. Only a part of her was in the frame. 'Nothing is complete, only a suggestion of what there is. There is an old Zen proverb: *A garden is not complete until nothing can be removed*.' He handed the camera back to me, 'You should study photography—you have a good eye.' A bell went off in the distance. 'Time for lunch,' the monk said as he stood, 'would you like to join me?'

'Sorry, I must go,' I said. 'Thank you.'

He bowed and said, 'So-re ma-de—until then.'

I hurried down the path. I was meeting Yasunari for lunch. We were going to Meigetsu-in, the hydrangea temple known for its splendid blue blossoms. The sky above was also a brilliant blue; the sun had melted the clouds into tufts of haze. I felt a flutter deep inside.

It was our last night in Kamakura. We returned to the inn in which we had two rooms separated by sliding shoji doors. It was late, and Yasunari walked me into my room, which was filled with the smell of straw from the tatami mats, pine from the pillars, and paper dust from the shoji doors. He pulled the mattress from the cupboard, arranged the rice husk pillows and a diaphanous quilt, below the folds of which, as though sheltered, he removed my clothes. My long hair tumbled down, covering my breasts. I don't know how long he sat opposite me. I closed my eyes; I was drained emotionally. When I finally opened them, I saw him leave through the shoji door.

I was glad that he had shown an interest in me. Though there was Mohan, of course, I had written to him before I left Bombay but hadn't given him my address in Kyoto. I wondered if I should write to him, and then decided maybe not. I didn't want to tell him about Yasunari, didn't want him to know I was glad to be here with him. This gladness made me realise how lonely I really was.

That night, alone in my small room, as I lay wakeful, my heart brimmed with all sorts of feelings. I stared at the clock on the wall; I could hear its slow ticking in my head. The smell of the night lingered in my dreams, not just of tatami mats and pine-pillars, but of something different: the whiff of shadows and anticipation and hope.

The Daruma's hollow eyes gleamed in the faint light of the morning. On a whim, I plucked it from the alcove and made a wish. Then, with a kohl pencil, I blackened one of its eyes. *Sore made*, I thought. *Until then.*

Kyoto, 2002

The newspaper reported on the typhoon that had hit the southern coast; discussed the tremors that we'd felt during the night.

Ojiisan inspected the wooden post in the corner of the room. 'There's a small tear here. Thankfully, the tremors were light.'

Obaasan asked me, 'Did you not hear the doors rattle, the floor tremble, the light bulb swing from side to side?'

'I was fast asleep,' I said.

'You must learn to sleep light, listen to the sounds.'

I heard the toast pop out of the toaster.

'Where's Yasunari?' Ojiisan asked.

'He came home late last night,' Obaasan replied.

Ojiisan grunted. 'He's drinking too much, and if you ask me, he's spending far too much time with Hiroo.'

Obaasan waved her hand at him. 'Let him be. He's working hard.'

'I work hard too!' Ojiisan wore an exasperated look on his face. 'I have got to fix our house. I noticed three of the wooden posts have deep gashes.'

'The house is too old to repair, Ojiisan.' Obaasan frowned. 'Yasunari said he would build us a solid steel and concrete house. It says in the papers that we should build houses with sturdy concrete foundations and strong walls.'

A shadow came over Ojiisan's face. 'I have to go now. Morita-san called this morning—a part of his house has collapsed. I told him many times to replace the old wooden posts. They had rotted.'

'I will get your breakfast,' Obaasan said.

'I will have breakfast with Morita-san. I don't think I will be back for lunch.'

After he left, I looked through my folder of photographs and papers. On my return from Kamakura, I decided not to return to Bombay with my uncle. I told him about my plans to stay and study photography. He was pleased with my decision and helped me to enroll in a photography course in Tokyo. He arranged a room for me at Sakura House, a dormitory for women. It was in Hongō, a short walk from the photography institute.

I would be leaving Kyoto soon.

Obaasan went into the garden to check the plants. The ground was covered with leaves and broken branches, and the ginkgo nuts were strewn under the tree. 'I'll help you, Obaasan,' I shouted. We spent the entire morning restoring the garden.

'We will clean up the rest later,' Obaasan said as she walked through the door. 'Let's go out for lunch. Ojiisan will not be back for some time.'

'It's still early, Obaasan.'

'Let's hanasanpo.'

'What?'

'Flower-walk. The ajisai are in full bloom in the park. We can cut across and go to the new French café on the other side; we can have an early lunch. I have to meet a friend after that and won't be back until the evening.'

Sunlight accentuated the uneven paving beneath our feet. Shadows of trees settled on the road, moving and shifting with the wind, and leaves and small branches were scattered everywhere. Despite the tremors, many people were out. I had brought my camera and snapped several pictures: two girls, perhaps sisters, in identical blue dresses, a young woman with a baby strapped to her back, a cluster of school children in uniforms, and amidst them, an elderly woman in yellow socks. There was something curiously simple about these people, nothing, no one, was incongruous; they all belonged. I was thinking of where I belonged; I always seemed to be out of place.

We entered the gates of the park, and further in, the hydrangea blossoms mirrored the azure sky: a blanket of blue and white flowers stretched beside the pathway and over the undulating mounds beyond. The blue flowers and the sky, wrapped in a mid-morning haze, merged in the distance, making the sky seem a part of the garden. Tumbled flowers covered the ground. Nothing, not even a tree or flower, grew in the garden by accident. Even the branches, fallen due to the tremors, appeared to be there by intent. We sat on a bench perched on a knoll to take in the remarkable view. Arranged on combed sand in front of us was an assemblage of bonsai.

'My mother taught me ikebana and bonsai,' Obaasan said. 'She was good.'

Her words took me by surprise; I hadn't seen any bonsai in her garden or flower arrangements in the house. Occasionally she bought potted flowering plants, which she set on the windowsill.

'I had many bonsai in the garden before,' she said, 'and Ojiisan liked the flowers I arranged in the house. Though, I gave it all up many years ago.' A frown crumpled Obaasan's face. 'I don't like the idea of cutting flowers and arranging them in a contrived way, nor do I like to prevent a plant from growing by throttling its roots with wires. Nature meant them to be free. Like them, I would like to be free.'

I pressed my hand on her shoulder. Changing the subject, she said, 'Do you know we have meanings for most of the flowers? Ajisai, these hydrangeas, is *pride*. The Sagiso flowers mean, *my thoughts flow into your dreams*. Kuchinashi, *secret love*, and Wasurenagusa—the forget-me-nots—is *true love*. Tsubaki is *longing*. I love Sayuri—the orange lily—though it means *hatred* or *revenge*. There are times, I must admit, I want to buy a half dozen pots of Sayuri and put them on the windowsill.'

She slapped her thighs with her hands, stood up abruptly. 'Let's go.' We walked across the park to the French café; we ordered croque monsieur and strawberry parfait. 'The house is so old now,' Obaasan said, 'but Ojiisan will never agree to build a new one. You saw the fuss he made about the water heater in the bathroom.'

'Yes, he won't agree,' I said, 'he is proud of the house.'

'He built it himself. We didn't have much money then. We put all our savings into it, and Ojiisan put his heart into it. But it's coming apart now; wooden houses need a lot of care and attention. Yasunari said a concrete house is better, easier to maintain, and will last longer.'

'I don't think Ojiisan will like Yasunari's ideas.'

'How well you know him. Yes, you are right. Yasunari's designs are a bit crazy, but his work is admired—recently, a magazine covered his work. He showed it to me but not to Ojiisan.' She wiped her lips with the napkin. 'This is delicious,' she said and pushed away the empty parfait glass. 'Some time back, a magazine approached Ojiisan to feature the houses he had built, but he refused them. He is a private person and doesn't like publicity.'

After lunch, Obaasan left to meet her friend, and I returned home. I made coffee and switched on the television. I watched Obaasan's favourite serial: it was about an alcoholic husband whose wife has an affair with a younger man. I understood why Obaasan watched such serials; there was a dream that they offered, a hidden crevice that she could sink into for exacting periods of time. Everything around her was so well orchestrated, set to tune, remote-controlled, and she moved about like a shadow with strings which, when pulled, would make her comply, conform, and be safe in a knot of rules.

'I'm home,' Ojiisan said as he walked in. 'Where's Obaasan?'

'Gone to meet her friend, she will be back in the evening.

Do you need anything?'

'I'm alright. I will go to the monastery for my Zen class,' Ojiisan said hastily.

Later, Obaasan returned with bags, and peeping out of one of them was the most brilliantly coloured flower—purple, indigo, and violet. 'Shikuramen,' she said. 'Is Ojiisan here?'

I said, 'Not yet. I thought you would be back later.'

'My friend's husband was unwell; she couldn't stay long, so we stopped for a quick tea, then I met my friend Katayama-san. We went to a shibori exhibition; he bought me flowers and a cake.' She hesitated. 'It's my birthday today.'

'Oh, I didn't know. I would have bought you a gift. I wish Ojiisan had told me.'

'He doesn't like to remember today.' She made tea and sat down beside me in front of the television. 'So, she returns to her husband? I thought she would.'

'Why would she? He is a drunkard; I think she should marry the young school teacher.'

'And then what? When they are married, he will start drinking and beating her. They are all alike.' She shook her head vigorously, and her grey hair tied into a knot at the nape of her neck, secured with a wooden comb, came loose. She removed the comb, tightened the knot, and put the comb back in her hair: it seemed to me as though she was upholding her life, securing it with that comb.

'Ojiisan isn't like that,' I said.

Obaasan narrowed her eyes. 'He had a frightful temper when he was younger. On the nights he had too much to drink, he would fight with me for no reason, and on occasion, he even slapped me.'

I was startled. 'I can't imagine him doing that.'

Obaasan waved a hand in the air. 'It's no serious matter, really; a familiar routine in a married woman's life. And Ojiisan had many disappointments after all. He had reasons to be angry, to be upset.' She gazed out of the window. 'Ojiisan's father was a carpenter and wanted his son to be a master craftsman—to build traditional houses. Ojiisan wanted to become a musician, though; he played drums very well.'

I could not understand how she, so humble in all her ways, could be so strong.

She turned her face to me. 'Now, where is Ojiisan? He has been gone since morning.'

'He came back for a bit but then went to his Zen class.'

'Zen class. I see. Is that what he told you?'

'Yes, he did say Zen class.'

'He has not gone to any Zen class. He always says this when he goes to see Yasuko.'

'Yasuko? Who is she?'

She didn't reply. She continued to watch the television serial intently. 'You are right,' she said. 'She should marry the school teacher.' Etched on her face was an expression of resignation.

It was late when Ojiisan returned.

'You could have telephoned,' Obaasan complained. 'We were waiting for you to have dinner.'

'I don't want dinner.'

'Ojiisan, at least have some of Obaasan's birthday cake,' I said.

'Good night,' Ojiisan replied and walked away.

After dinner, I took a cup of tea outside. Obaasan sat down and looked up at the clear sky. Her face was a little flushed as she said, 'Shikuramen flowers fade fast. The leaves start to yellow and fall off, and then the plant will wither and return to the soil. Not any different from relationships, unless fleeting, or founded on unselfish love, or better still, a tragedy.'

She started singing *Shikuramen No Kaori*—the scent of cyclamen. It was a popular song, and I had heard it before. It was about the lonely scent of the purple shikuramen that floats in vain as the loved one leaves the lover, and time, like a child that never tires, passes them by.

Dusklight caught the cobweb of wrinkles at the base of her neck. She spoke in a soft voice, 'Yasuko was his girlfriend. He had been seeing her for many years. She was thirteen years younger than him. Of course, she was beautiful. She was a musician; she played the koto. Ojiisan repaired her house, and that's how their friendship started. Poor woman, she died in a car accident; her koto smashed beside her. Coincidentally, she died on my birthday, and Ojiisan was never the same again. He started living in the past. He visits her grave often and sits with her for hours. He says he can hear music.'

Obaasan stared at the spot where the moon should have been, though there was no moon, just a blotch in the sky. The tear stains on her cheek lit only by the stars.

Obaasan looked elegant in a cotton yukata dyed the colour of deer skin, with a pattern of delicate fronds of varying shades of green, even purple; it complimented the deep purple obi tied around her waist and fastened with an ivory clasp. Her hair was tied in a bun at the nape of her neck and secured with a jade pin. She wore no jewellery besides these, and her face was devoid of make-up. Ojiisan wore a deep brown yukata with a black sash. They both wore geta on their feet. I wore the only saree I had with me. It belonged to my aunt, a Kanchipuram silk in the colours of a peacock's tail. It was morning, and we were going to the family grave for ohaka mairi—to pay respect to the loved ones who had passed away. It was August and time for the Obon festival.

Carrying food, fruits, flowers, and incense sticks, we took the bus to the cemetery not too far away. Countless tombs made of grey stone, not individual but familial, populated the small enclosure dotted with trees, shrubs, and small gardens. Stone paths washed by the wind and late rain teemed with the singing of insects. Ojiisan's family tomb was secluded amidst a grove of cedar trees. Obaasan washed the tomb with a pail of water. She arranged the flowers, and as the smoke curled upward from the bundle of incense sticks she had lit, she offered food and fruits to the departed. She closed her eyes and prayed, as did Ojiisan. They talked aloud to their ancestors' spirits, expressed gratitude, and even shared with them titbits of news about this and that. I shut my eyes, and took refuge in the dimness behind my eyelids and talked to my mother, my father, wordlessly. I told them about Yasunari. *Sore made—until then.*

Only a blur of pale yellow was visible across the darkening sky. The cherry trees on the street were just a swell of grey shadows. Obaasan lit a small bonfire in front of the house. 'For the ritual of mukaebi,' she told me, 'to guide the spirits back home.' Over the next couple of days, she prepared shōjin ryōri—a vegetarian meal made with local and seasonal ingredients chosen for their subtle taste, colour, and texture. She made rolled yuba with sweet miso, konjac, local potatoes, carrots, and shiitake mushrooms, tofu, tempura, and vegetables in a variety of sauces, sprinkled with seeds, and rice.

She planned each meal to balance the power of five, to appeal to the senses: the five colours (white, green, yellow, black, red), the five flavours (sweet, sour, salty, bitter, umami), the five ways of cooking (raw, stirred, boiled, fried, steamed), and the five elements (fruits, legumes, grain, vegetables, condiments), that contained distinctive energies good for health and well-being.

On Okuribi, the last day of the Obon festival, large bonfires lit up the sky to guide the spirits to the netherworld. Obaasan took me to the Bon-odori—a group dance performed on a side lane leading to the nearby temple. She wore a simple shibori yukata in shades of indigo, and I, a short green yukata worn over trousers. Amidst the pulsating beats of taiko drums, the song of Sōran Bushi, and the paper lanterns rising above us, we danced in the memory of those that had come before. Their spirits danced with us as a flock of birds crossed the twilight sky on their way back home.

* * *

Yasunari was moving to Tokyo; he had joined a prestigious architecture firm—'Working with them will be good for me,' he'd said.

'Of course, it will be good for *you*,' Ojiisan taunted. 'You will build more glass boxes and make more money.'

'It's as though you are happy to see him go, Ojiisan,' Obaasan protested. She was miserable.

Later that day, Ojiisan confided in Obaasan, 'It is good that Yasu-chan is leaving. He will concentrate on his work and won't be around that Hiroo so much.'

The day Yasunari left, Ojiisan lingered in the doorway—a naked look in his eyes, like the empty hollows of the sukiya addressing the passing of a season.

The next day, Ojiisan made plans to see the film *Tora! Tora! Tora!* that was showing at a local cinema house. Obaasan refused to come with us.

'Is it because she misses Yasunari?' I asked Ojiisan.

'She doesn't like war movies,' he said.

The film was about the Japanese attack on Pearl Harbor. I didn't enjoy it either; it was too long.

It was late when we made our way home. I stopped in front of a quaint little restaurant that displayed, in a glass case, a selection of donburi—rice bowls. I was hungry.

'Shall we eat here, Ojiisan?' I asked.

'Let's go home,' he replied. 'I'm sure Obaasan will have cooked up a spread as she usually does when she's alone. She will be rather upset if we have already eaten.'

Obaasan hadn't made dinner; she was not in the mood she had told Ojiisan, so he ordered soba noodles from a shop on the main road. We sat in the back garden after dinner. Obaasan didn't talk; she looked pensive.

Ojiisan talked about the film. 'Tora was a Japanese code word,' he told me. It meant lightning attack. He talked about the ingenuity of Admiral Isoroku Yamamoto's plan and how they had caught the Americans off guard. 'It was a masterstroke,' he said, which had transformed Japan into a world power.

Obaasan looked forlorn. 'Don't forget what Admiral Yamamoto said about waking the sleeping giant.' She sighed. 'If Pearl Harbor hadn't happened, they would never have bombed Hiroshima.' I noticed the tears that had sprung to her eyes.

Outside, from the street, the yaki-imo man rang his bell and shouted, 'Yaki-imo, yaki-imo, yaki-imoooo.' Obaasan's spirits soared at once, and Ojiisan hurried to the gate and returned with a paper parcel containing several roasted sweet potatoes. Obaasan peeled the scorched skin and then consumed the yaki-imo with capfuls of warm tea. Her face turned as bright as the moon, tranquil.

Tokyo, 2003

It was a simple ceremony, the day I left for Tokyo. I knelt down on the tatami floor and Ojiisan and Obaasan knelt facing me. With our hands on the floor, we bowed. No words were spoken.

Yasunari stayed with his parents, Keiko and Shigeru, in Mitaka, a distant suburb. I met them in their home only once when they invited me for dinner. I met Yasunari at Shinjuku Station, and we had taken the train to Mitaka; his house was not too far from the station.

His mother was stylish, courteous, but aloof. His father was considerate and kind. 'Your uncle and I have been friends for many years,' he said. 'You're welcome to stay with us anytime you want.'

'Yes, you should stay here,' Yasunari smiled. 'Let me show you the house,' he offered.

His mother frowned. 'I will show her,' she quickly said.

The house was a long, black, rectangular block with skylights. It had a red front door but nothing else on the front façade. The tall glass wall at the back overlooked the garden, which was a forest of trees. Inside, the house had lace curtains dividing the spaces, velvet sofas, glass chandeliers, porcelain dolls, and a courtyard with a contemporary sculpture at its centre.

'Yasunari built this house, but I did the interiors myself,' Keiko-san said. 'Of course, Yasunari hates it. He likes modern stuff with clean lines and without ornamentation.'

Her bedroom was like a house in itself: it had a lounge facing another courtyard filled with sand, and on it, a large metal tree, its leaves dancing in the breeze. Beyond it was the most elaborate bathroom I had ever seen. It had a sunroom with a glass roof, a bathtub shaped like a lotus in pink-veined marble with golden faucets, and mirrors on all sides. There were soft towels, snow-like soaps, salts, oils, and perfumes of all kinds. Next to the lace-curtained window was a large marble vase with silk flowers.

'I copied it from a design magazine,' Keiko-san confided. 'Yasunari doesn't like it—he likes clean lines,' she repeated.

'Come, let's go into the garden,' Yasunari said when we returned to the living room.

'Don't go yet, I'm serving dinner now. Yasunari likes Italian food,' she said to me.

She served dinner soon enough: tomato soup, seafood spaghetti, and a large salad. I felt uncomfortable because she seemed to be in a terrible hurry. She scowled as Yasunari spooned pasta onto my plate. We had fruit and a platter of cheese for dessert, and soon after, she said, 'You have such a long way to go. I don't want to delay you.'

'I will drive you back,' Yasunari offered. 'It's still early. We can have coffee somewhere.'

'Oh, coffee would be nice,' I said hastily.

'You have an early start tomorrow Yasu-chan,' his mother said. 'Why don't I drop her off at the train station.' She turned to me. 'You can manage from there, can't you?'

'Yes, of course.' I got the feeling she didn't like me very much. 'Thank you for dinner. You have a lovely house,' I said, and we left.

Her house was the antithesis of my modest abode. Sakura House was a four-storied structure with rooms to let on the upper two floors, a fancy spa, and a French café, which served coffee and a variety of French desserts, occupied the bottom floors.

I shared the dormitory with seven girls: three from Singapore, two from Hong Kong, and two from Malaysia. They avoided me, referred to me as the immigrant girl, the girl from elephant land, so I kept away from them. The girls took turns cooking dinner—the only meal that they had together in the communal kitchen with a single window measuring one-foot-by-one-foot. These small windows seemed to have been mass-ordered: all eight bedrooms had them; they were just broad enough to stick your head out of. The shared bathroom had a similar window. It was not surprising, therefore, for the girls to chatter about a dream house full of windows: floor to ceiling windows, wall-to-wall windows, roof windows, corner windows, smiling windows, happy windows, much like the urchin in *Dodes'ka-den*, and Malli.

On one wall of the kitchen hung several charms thought to bring good fortune and keep away the evil eye. They all belonged to the landlady, Sakura-san. Besides these, there were posters of music stars, models, a to-do memo, a medical prescription, and a diet chart itemising the calories in various vegetables, meats, fruits, and drinks. The refrigerator contained personal items: a variety of sauces, pickles, fruit juices, and chocolates.

Each one had a label with a girl's name: Lee. Tang. Lim. Chan. Leung. Wong and Ng. I put my name on the things that belonged to me. It felt like I was marking my territory, my own little island in a vast ocean, both unknown and indifferent to me.

Sakura-san was a wealthy, well-travelled woman. She must have been about fifty and lived next door to the dormitory in an old house that had belonged to her grandparents. She used to be a film star, the girls had told me; an enchantress with a slim body, a dazzling smile, and huge, pool-like eyes. Now her body was swollen, and her eyes were fretted with creases; her skin was a pale blue arabesque of veins, and she was always dressed in colourful, flamboyant robes. She was also superstitious.

Sakura-san met with us every other Saturday in the communal kitchen to discuss our requirements: repairs, rent, rules. One time, when someone asked her to replace the one-foot-by-one-foot windows, she had said, 'Feng shui: there is a lot of good energy in the dormitory, mostly in the kitchen. That's why we have the small windows. You don't want all your good fortune to fly away through large windows, do you?'

I clung tight to my small fortunes: the one-foot-by-one-foot ones.

Never had I looked forward to anything with such anticipation. I couldn't calm my throbbing excitement on the first day of the photography class, but the thrill I had felt faded soon enough. I had hoped to make new friends, but no one was particularly friendly. The lessons were not easy, and all the course material was in Japanese, which I still couldn't read fluently. The instructor had given me a list of books in English, and so I spent considerable time in the university library, alone. Sadness grew on my skin like scabies, and I scratched away incessantly at the weariness and gloom I felt.

There were sixteen students in the class. We had lessons for two hours in the morning, after which we were asked to shoot pictures on our own. Sometimes the instructor accompanied us. When he explained the view in front of us, I couldn't focus on what he said, it was too technical, and when he asked me a question, my answer was usually rather inappropriate. The other students were all amused by what I said, except Ryu Watanabe. He was indifferent, preoccupied with whatever he saw through the camera lens. However, occasionally, his tentative smile revealed that he was aware of my turmoil, of my strange sort of loneliness, but could do nothing about it.

Most of the time, the instructor was not with us. The other students paired up or went out in groups. I once again resorted to my old hobby—the exercise I had learnt in the creative writing workshop back in Bombay of tailing a curious person. It gave me something to do. Moreover, I got to know the bus routes, the underground and overground train terminals, and the street layout better than before.

Sakura-san invited me to tea one afternoon. I was surprised, and so were the girls. They had not been to her house, they said, which made me a bit anxious. She was dressed in a bright purple robe with splashes of yellow. I had expected her house to be exuberant, like her, but I was mistaken. It seemed to be just the way her grandparents had left it, and there was not a thing that was modern or fancy. We sat in the veranda at the back, a friendly poodle by her feet. She asked me a stream of questions, which thankfully, were not too personal —*Is it hot in India? Do elephants still roam wild? Is the food too spicy? Are there hundreds of gods?*—and I fed her curiosity as concisely as I could.

The housekeeper brought us tea, a bowl of mikan—sweet, seedless oranges, and wedges of strawberry cheesecake. Sakura-san said, 'That's got cheese and egg. Is that okay?' I hesitated, and before I could reply, she turned to the housekeeper and said, 'She's from India. She may not eat that. Take the cheesecake away.' Sakura-san selected a mikan from the bowl; she did not tear the peel apart but gently opened it, petal by petal, like a flower. She offered it to me and then poured some tea. It was a muggy afternoon.

'I planted all these bamboo trees,' she said, pointing to clusters of shrubs growing all over the garden. 'They promote good fortune; they are called nanten. It is a play on words: nanten—*Nan wo tenzuru*—which means, *Problems which turn for the better*.'

There was something unusually tranquil about those little trees. Even the sound they made as they swayed in the breeze was soothing.

'I have not been so fortunate with husbands though,' Sakura-san said, lighting a cigarette. 'I was married three times. The first was a Japanese artist, five years younger; he was only twenty-two. He was moody, unstable, and drank too much. I smoked too much, and one evening he went to get me a pack of cigarettes and never returned. Then I married a Thai businessman from Bangkok. He owned a hotel and was wealthy enough to afford a house of his own, but he chose to live with his family. I was his third wife. His mother was cantankerous and too possessive of her son, and he was rather old. Six months later, I returned home. My last husband was an American, a hippie, really. We lived in San Francisco. We did fun things at first, and we were happy and free, at least I thought we were. Then I got bored of all the contrived togetherness and happiness; I needed to be alone, needed to be truly free. I had the perfect reason when my grandfather died, and so I returned to care for his old wife. That was fifteen years ago.'

Suddenly, powdery rain descended from the sky. A spray of wetness touched my face. Sakura-san let out a high-pitched squeal of laughter. 'If you ask me, despite my age, I really don't know the definition of happiness. Each time I married,

I assumed it was because of love, and that I would be happy. Sadly, I was unhappy.' She sighed, looked down at the poodle by her feet. 'Now I have Suki,' she pointed to the dog, 'and all these musical bamboo trees. We are lucky and happy.' The nanten bushes tinkled in the wind, she smiled, 'Do you know your uncle got Suki for me?'

'How did you meet him?'

'I met him at Shigeru Hara's house before I went to Bangkok. I kept in touch with him all this time; we are good friends.'

I reached out impulsively and clutched her hand. I knew who she was—she was S-san. I blurted out about the letters I wrote to her and at once felt embarrassed.

She held my hand in both of hers. 'Your uncle sent me photos of you. I'm so glad I finally got to meet you.' She glanced at her wristwatch. 'Oh no! Look at the time. I have an appointment at the salon!' She stroked her brown hair. 'I am colouring it red, the colour of the season. Do you think it will suit me?'

'Yes,' I said. I thought that was the only polite response.

Then, as abruptly as the rain had started, it was time to go. As I prepared to leave, I glanced up, and to my right, I could see the dormitory kitchen, the one-foot-by-one-foot window was wide open.

Yasunari had bought me a Nikon camera. Being in Tokyo at the same time, I felt closer to him. In my free time, whenever I had it, I sent cards to Obaasan and Ojiisan, and I wrote to my aunt and uncle, told them about S-san. Now and then, she invited me to tea or dinner. Sometimes she took me shopping. I was glad. Yasunari was busy, and we hadn't seen each other in over two months. We spoke on the phone sometimes but not often. His absence stirred up my feelings for him. I was delighted and relieved when he called and asked me to dinner; he had moved to a flat in Ebisu.

I told S-san about Yasunari. 'He's a nice young man,' she said, 'and very talented. I haven't seen him in a long time, though.'

I didn't go to the studio the next day; S-san took me shopping instead. She got me a new blouse and a pair of fitted trousers. I don't usually wear make-up, yet she bought me a pale shade of lipstick and a jar of creamy blush-on. She had also booked me an appointment for a fancy hair treatment at the salon below the dormitory.

I was ready early. S-san had asked me to pack my toiletries in my handbag, just in case it got too late to return to the dormitory. 'I will worry,' she said, 'and give me his phone number.' On S-san's suggestion, I had bought a box of chouquettes, filled with custard and dipped in chocolate, from the French café below. I winked at the Daruma doll I had set on the windowsill, and I was off.

Yasunari opened the door but looked startled. 'You are way too early,' he laughed and hugged me. I caught my breath as he drew me inside. 'I only just got back from work; I must get changed,' he said. He didn't seem to notice my hair or my new clothes, but I was so pleased to see him that it didn't bother me. Yasunari left me in the hall and darted into the bedroom. It was a studio apartment with an open plan kitchen and hardly any furniture. On the side-table was a model of a building: a white rectangular block with panels of glass on two sides as well as on top.

'It's Ojiisan's new house,' Yasunari said from behind. I turned, and standing next to Yasunari was another man. He was older, tall, and lean, and his face was creaseless as though the skin over it had been stretched too tight. He had on a bright magenta silk shirt, and his long, dark hair was tied in a ponytail.

'Ravi de vous rencontrer,' he held out his hand in a flourish.

'This is Hiroo,' Yasunari said.

I bowed. 'Pleased to meet you.'

Yasunari clasped his hands together. 'Ojiisan has finally agreed. Soon, I'm going to Kyoto to start work on the house, and Ojiisan and Obaasan will move to a temporary place for six months or so. The new house is prefabricated and won't take long to build; it should be ready before winter. I am famished, let's eat,' Yasunari said. 'Hiroo is an excellent cook—he's made fish, French-style.'

After dinner, which was rather hopeless, Yasunari and Hiroo sat on the sofa whilst I sat on the only other chair, facing them. It was still early, but I was beginning to get impatient; I was waiting for Hiroo to leave. To prompt his departure, I asked him, 'Do you live close by?'

'He lives here—with me,' Yasunari said and rested his head in the crook of Hiroo's arm. He then talked in detail about their plans for the winter. 'We are going to the south of France where there's good weather to drive in.'

Hiroo snuggled up close to Yasunari and kissed his cheek. 'Je vous adore.'

I felt like an intruder, and so I left rather brusquely.

At Ebisu subway station, I noticed a woman with a plaster on her left ear. She must have been in her mid-thirties. She was lean and tall, with spindly legs, and wore black samurai pants and a loose indigo shirt. Her long hair, permed in wild curls, with hints of blue, was coiled on top of her head and secured with a stick. She wore no make-up except the dark kohl that rimmed her eyes. It seemed to me as though she had taken great pains to appear cool and wacky; that perhaps she had something to hide or forget. For all her composure, she was clumsy and kept dropping the large envelope she held in her hand. I was rather clumsy myself, and this fact had drawn my attention to her.

Out of habit, I followed her onto the Hibiya line and selected a seat not too far from hers. She fidgeted the whole journey, moving her legs and adjusting her clothes. I got off at Ginza station and took the Ginza line. This time I sat right next to her and could hear her breathing heavily, sighing occasionally. She got off at Asakusa, and I followed her down the street. She entered the Saké Art House and perched herself on a barstool. The place was both a bar and an art gallery, a fusion of traditional Japanese and twenties Bauhaus style. Paintings hung on the two exposed concrete walls. Oddly, the bar stocked all kinds of alcohol but not saké. Most of the people there—barring a few business men in sharp suits—were dressed in casual, hip clothing. The three women in kimono, who had possibly stopped for a drink after a visit to the temple, appeared totally out of place.

I sat on a stool at the other end of the bar. She ordered a beer and looked anxiously towards the door. She glanced around, and then her eyes rested on me. She smiled, shouted across, 'You I see before. You from train, ne? You follow me?' I was startled. She laughed at my expression. She picked up her bottle of beer and sat on the stool next to me. 'Beeru, okay?' I nodded; she ordered me a bottle of Asahi and asked if I spoke Japanese.

'Yes, I do,' I replied.

She spoke in Japanese with a spattering of English. She had a sweet, caressing voice. 'I noticed you on the train,' she said, 'because of your lovely big eyes and the colour of your skin, like roasted almonds.' She held my hand. 'Such small hands.'

I began to feel nervous, but I wanted to know more about her. 'What happened to your ear?' I asked.

'Oh, that,' she touched her earlobe, 'it's nothing really.' She laughed. 'Did you think someone had bitten it off?' I was embarrassed, but she gave my hand a gentle, reassuring squeeze. I pulled my hand away. She laughed again. 'You're so cute.' She leant towards me. 'Are you a virgin? Have you done it?' She laughed out loud at my expression. 'I was like you—what do you say in English, in-no-cen-t.' She continued, 'My parents were simple farmers, and I spent most of my childhood amidst the wild grass—I was wild. My mother was old-fashioned, domineering even, and there was so much confusion in my mind: my soul was troubled. I ran away from my home in Okinawa when I was just fifteen and came to Tokyo. I wanted to experience life, all its facets, good and bad, so I slept with men I met, young, old, many of them boring. When I was your age, I was already pregnant twice. I had two abortions. My family, my friends—all said I was an easy woman. They were so hateful, but I didn't care; there is more hatred in this world than love anyway. So I became like a zakuro. You know zakuro?' I shook my head. She thought for a bit, 'Like po-me-gra-nate. Hard skin on the outside with nuggets of juicy wisdom inside.' She reached out and caressed my face. 'Be tough and love life.'

I heard someone call out. The woman turned and waved her hand as a young man walked towards her.

He caressed her injured ear. 'She thinks you bit my ear off,' she said, and they laughed.

'I must go,' I said and slid off the stool.

'Wait...' She took a business card from her bag and gave it to me. It was square and black with a sketch of a dense cluster of fine grass in white, and barely visible amidst them, the word *artist*. 'Chahikigusa,' she said, 'it means wild oats. My father called me that—chahikigusa.' On the reverse of the card was etched her name: Akiko, phone number, and address. She asked me for my number; I gave it to her. 'I'll call you,' she said. 'See you. Bye.'

'Bye,' I said and then rushed towards the door.

I hurried back to the station and took the train to Ginza,

changed to the Marunouchi line, and returned to Hongō. Just as I was passing S-san's house, she bundled out of the door, wrapped her arm around my shoulder, and ushered me inside. She made tea, and we sat together on the veranda. She had telephoned Yasunari, she said, and he had let her know that I had left a long time ago. 'He was worried, you left so abruptly. What happened?' As briefly as I could, I told her about Yasunari and Hiroo. 'Nan wo tenzuru—' she repeated '*—problems which turn for the better.*' The nanten bushes tinkled in the wind.

I returned to my room and sat on the bed. I didn't think about Yasunari; I thought, instead, of the strange woman and wrote about her in my diary. I drew a large pomegranate, cut in half, numerous plump nuggets inside, and wrote against it in capital letters—BE ONE. I had no clue about her injured ear; her hairdresser must have gashed it, I concluded.

The next morning, as I woke, I saw the Daruma on the windowsill. I jumped out of bed, crushed the doll in my hands, the papier-mâché ripped, and bits of it fell to the floor. The eyes, the black and the white one, now apart, mocked me. I picked them up and stuffed them into the bin. One of my small fortunes, a one-foot-by-one-foot one, was mislaid during that night.

* * *

The photography studio was closed. It wasn't a break—we were required to compile a photo-essay of street scenes during this time. The students had been divided into pairs, and my partner was Ryu Watanabe. He had worked at a bank, he told me, but had given it up to study photography much to his father's apprehension. His mother, however, supported his decision. 'You have to do what you have to do, when you have to do it,' she had said. And so he did.

Ryu was quiet and kept to himself. The other students went out for lunch together whilst Ryu sat on the bench in the garden and ate from the bento box his mother had prepared for him. I ate my packed lunch hastily in the corridor outside the classroom. We were both different from the rest of the students, Ryu was much older, and I was foreign, so I was surprised when Ryu asked me hesitantly, 'We sit, you like, with me? By our selves, you-me eat?' As we sat under the maple tree, Ryu said, 'I teach more Japanese to you. You-me English teach?' He had such beautiful hands.

Although he was quiet and restrained, when he chose to, he talked a lot. Some of the things he did with his hands and face as he talked reminded me of someone else: he pulled at his ear lobe when deep in thought, as though it had slipped down a little and he had to adjust the balance of his face, and when he was thrilled about something, he crossed his wrists and locked his fingers in a tight grasp. I wondered who it was he reminded me of. My father? My brother? I couldn't recollect. Although I did remember the way my brother tweaked his nose with his fingers when he had forgotten something important. My uncle did that too, and sometimes my aunt jokingly imitated him.

Ryu lived close to the institute, so we met early each morning in front of the bank where he had worked and wandered around taking pictures. Ryu spent considerable time on each shot; he was particular and patient. He took me to a street that he liked a lot: a narrow lane that wound up to a shrine, of which, only a glimpse could be seen. On either side of the lane were low, tile-roofed houses with verandas screened by reed and bamboo blinds. The latticed panels afforded hints of the interior, and as the light changed—much like the patterns made by the glass pieces in a kaleidoscope—so did the layers within. They opened my eyes to the world of semi-ness: semi-permanent, semi-enclosed, semi-public, semi-visible, semi-coloured, semi-light, semi-dark, all of it.

I took pictures and showed them to Ryu. 'They are all flat,' he said, shaking his head. 'You must compose each image like an onion, in many layers, peel by peel, all together.' He told me about omote and ura—the front and back, and their importance in photography: the sky became a backdrop for the mountains, and the hills, the background for the forests, and so on. Omote-ura was not just about connections, but about character as well, he told me. Omote was formal and precise, ura the opposite, and depth from the front to the back was vital. 'If you get this right, your photo will be very good.' Oku—the innermost, was equally important, he said. It gave direction to the front-to-back movement, starting from the brighter and formal front and progressively reaching the dark, intimate interior. It was like a narrow path in a forest leading to a glimpse of a lake. The tighter the space, the more remote the oku, the view would appear deep and yet close. 'If you get this right, your photo will invoke feelings hidden inside your oku.'

Later, in the days I got to know him better, I noticed that he disliked anything of lasting beauty. Not that he didn't accept beauty, but he didn't like the idea of it lasting and used this as a shield to protect himself from himself. 'Who I am is not who I was, and who I will be in the future is not who I am today,' he said. 'I will change, and everything about me, around me, will too.' He was not very keen, therefore, on architecture, printed words, or recorded music—all of which would outlast their moment. He preferred spoken words, sung or played music, flowers that faded in a matter of days, spaces that changed continually dependent on the light and movement through them. Ruins were different, he said—they were the remains of something that had not lasted. When I argued with him that a photograph, a documented scene or memory, was no different from a book or recorded music, he replied, 'It depends on the photograph. It can be like a painting that reveals itself in different ways each time you look at it.' I disagreed, but I let it be, he was too firm in his belief, and I didn't want to tarnish that. Besides, I remembered what Malli had said about the beauty of things that died suddenly; I had agreed with her.

Ryu took me to Chōshi—the easternmost town along the Pacific Ocean—to watch the rising sun. We hired a car and left late in the afternoon with no intention of missing the early sunrise the next morning. Ryu had booked us rooms in a quaint inn. 'You will like it,' he said, 'it is old.'

Stepping through a narrow latticed door, I entered a small tatami room. At the centre was a quilt-covered table, and on the wall, a little window rose from the floor reaching only halfway up, and through it, I could see a pristine garden. I couldn't see the whole garden when I was standing, only a shallow glimpse of green at the floor level, but when I sat down at the table, I could see it in all its loveliness. The room, lit by the light from the garden window, was intimate and warm. Beyond, a corridor led inwards and deep into a courtyard. Ryu said excitedly, 'Look, this is the kind of oku I told you about. It's like peeling an onion, layer after layer.'

After dinner, we went for a stroll. The darkening sky, the crashing waves, the efforts of a bird flying against the wind, all these persisted as before in a timeless sequence. 'You were born in Bombay?' Ryu asked. I shook my head but didn't say any more. I didn't want him to feel sorry for me, and I didn't want him to be kind to me just because of it. Ryu seemed to understand. He said, 'People, too, have an omote, an ura, and an oku. Omote, our front, is what we reveal to people, and our ura is what we let our closest friends see. But deep within us, in our oku, we have feelings, memories, that no one can see and at times not even ourselves.' He talked about himself. His father had an old copy of *National Geographic* that contained a photo essay on quaint locomotives. He had wanted to be an engineer, had wanted to design trains. He became a train driver instead. 'Some people don't get to be who they want to be,' Ryu said, 'but I will be a good photographer, and I will go to America and work for *National Geographic*. I will travel and make lots of money, and my father will be happy.' He held my hand to reassure himself. 'I will change,' he said under his breath. The wind whistled in the distance, flute-like, and breathless.

At 5 a.m. the next morning, Ryu set up his tripod by the ocean. We waited, hand-in-hand, our omote-ura and oku bared, to greet the morning sun.

* * *

I was with S-san more often now: she took me to quaint Japanese restaurants, art and craft museums, to Mt. Fuji, Yokohama, and Hakone, where she had an old friend. 'Matsumoto-san is a famous potter,' she told me. 'He's eccentric, moody, and easily annoyed, but you will like him. He knows a lot of English and goes to America to give lectures on the history of Japanese art. His wife left him many years ago, she lives in Chicago now, and both their sons live there too. He lives alone and uses only one part of the house, and the rest is locked away, so he will have to open and air two rooms for us.'

I called my aunt; I hadn't spoken to her in some time. She was happy to hear from me and asked if I was eating well, if I was not too lonely, and when I would come and see her. I told her excitedly about S-san and all the things we did together. 'Why are you spending so much time with her?' She asked.

She sounded despondent, and I didn't understand why.

A few days before we left for Hakone, S-san took me to a Noh drama. Mishima, its director, had given her complimentary passes. They had been in drama school together, she told me, he had continued with theatre, and she had pursued film. Having learned Bharatanatyam and some Kathakali, I was keen to see Noh. There are many similarities between Kathakali and Kabuki, a form of theatre developed later, but which borrowed from Noh.

The Noh drama was grim and tough to comprehend, though there was something powerful in the orchestrated gestures—the masked expressions, and sudden stillness—that left me all together sad and tired. Afterwards, we had dinner with Mishima in a nearby restaurant. I told him what I thought about the drama, and he laughed. 'At least you are honest—I like that. Many can't appreciate Noh, though they pretend they do. Let me explain; it may help you understand. Noh drama has two concepts: monomane, the portrayal of a legend or event through words, song, music, action. It is not merely imitation, though, but a likeness, which makes it beautiful. Yūgen, however, is the core spirit of Noh. It is dark, mysterious, obscure, something that can't be revealed by words. Yūgen is something that you feel, not just glimpse. It is the moment a boat disappears over the horizon, the ripples in the water when a stone strikes it, the gossamer curtain flying in the wind. Think of haiku: it has few words and yet a vast absence of them. It is this absence of words, the emptiness, that sparks a deep feeling, this is yūgen. The most enjoyable part of the

Noh play, of course, is the stop-action: the stillness, the void. This was used in traditional Japanese art as well. You must have seen scrolls that are intricately painted, but some parts are left bare, vague, elusive. This is yūgen.'

I was confused with the new words he spoke of. In the end, for me, everything simmered down to the simple omote-ura-oku idea. What I saw, what I could sense, and the unseen feelings within. I had an omote-ura-oku, and with all the new information I received, I saw more, sensed more, and tried not to untangle the forgotten feelings deep within. I let them be.

I had perched Akiko's business card on my bookshelf so I wouldn't misplace it; I had hoped she would call, but she hadn't. Surely she had forgotten about our chance encounter, I thought and left it at that. On some days, I felt a strong urge to call her, but I didn't; I was shy and unsure. What would I say to her? Therefore, I was surprised, though glad, when she called and asked me to meet her at a café in Harajuku.

She was dressed once more in black samurai pants with an orange shirt. Her wild hair was left loose, her ear had now healed, and there was no longer a plaster over it. After coffee, she took me to her house-cum-studio, which was small yet spacious. The living room was painted black with fine white lines drawn on the walls, much like her business card. Fixed on a dazzling white, freestanding wall, were photographs and sketches. She was a graphic artist, she told me, and painted greeting and wedding cards, but was known more for her murals in offices, galleries, and restaurants, and her black-and-white photography. She showed me some of her work; they were fine ink sketches, dense, incomplete, and they appeared to be a detailed elaboration of a part of an image. Traditional Japanese art was all about bareness; there were no empty spaces here. When I asked her about this, she said, 'Around you, clutter everywhere, see. Life is a puzzle of people, things, and happenings, and they change from one situation to another. They are always incomplete, somewhere, sometime, somehow. My drawings zoom in on that clutter.' She showed me some of her photos. 'I sketch from actual photographs,' she added, 'my sketches are real.'

I asked her about her ear, and she laughed out loud. 'I fix a plaster on my skin where it is visible and change it daily. It's —you could say—my jewellery, it reassures me. It's strange, people notice physical pain, hurt, injury, and at once sympathise, even strangers, but they don't care for or notice emotional pain.' She had a plaster on her thumb that day.

It was cloudy when S-san and I drove to Hakone; the sun oozed from the petulant sky and covered the trees on either side with a hazy mist. Although it was afternoon, there was a chill in the air. We reached Matsumoto-san's house in just two hours, having stopped for a quick lunch on the way. He was in the garden, feeding the ducks in the pond. He was rather old and dressed in an ochre-brown yukata, the colour of autumn leaves. His rambling house cast a perfect shadow across the water. He walked over to us and bowed, as did we. 'You have changed the colour of your hair,' he said to S-san.

'The colour of the season,' she said. 'Do you like it?'

Matsumoto-san clicked his tongue. 'It reminds me of a desert flower, as does the rest of you.' His eyes travelled over her floral robe: crimson, red, and vermillion.

'Your tongue hasn't changed at all,' she said, laughing. 'It's as sharp as ever.'

Midori-san, a middle-aged woman, brought us a tray of tea; she set it on a stone table beneath the Chinese flame tree, its leaves gold and red in the setting sun. Matsumoto-san served the tea ceremoniously. The bowl I held in my hands was exquisite: stone grey with flecks of brown, the earth lending its colours to it.

I went for a stroll in the garden, so S-san and Matsumoto-san could catch up in my absence. It was dusk, and I could hear the twittering of birds returning home. Wild grass grew in dense bundles around the pond and the rays of the evening sun filtered through the trees, speckling the grass with light and dark shadows. The cicada had started its song. I sat down on a smooth boulder and listened to its cry. White flowers grew in clusters—as though carefully arranged—all around the rock.

'Don't!' I heard a hoarse shout and turned to see Matsumoto-san hurrying towards me, S-san in tow. 'That boulder is not to be sat on,' he said with a frown. I stood up hurriedly and apologised. 'I brought this rock all the way from Hokkaido. Look how beautiful it is, so smooth, and it has all the tones of grey. It is only to be admired from afar.'

He bent down and straightened some of the wildflowers I had trampled on, and then, standing up, he clasped his hands together. 'Come, let's have dinner.'

Dinner was an array of vegetables, which Matsumoto-san had carefully selected for their colour and texture. Midori-san served them either raw or lightly sautéed with bowls of rice. We ate at the table on the back veranda where Matsumoto-san and S-san talked about old times; I was quiet. The wind rustled through the nanten grove, and a bird gave its last call. Suddenly, the wind paused, S-san and Matsumoto-san were silent, the cicada rested, and the birds had reached home. I held my breath. It was like the stop-action in a Noh drama; I could feel the brief yawn of space and time. It was a dark night, but surprisingly, there were no stars in the sky. The crescent moon was all but a sliver, deserted, but when I looked at it again, I could see its ghost just below, like a half-shut eye. It made me think of my aunt. Was she unwell? Was she lonely, like the moon? I felt an unstoppable need to see her.

I didn't sleep well that night and woke early. Numerous tufts of faint clouds blotched the deep-blue sky and what seemed to be a dense mist rose over the hills in the distance. I followed a gravel path down the hill; the grass was still wet from the morning dew, and the cobwebs were quivering in the breeze. I saw a line of ants moving small clumps of mud. I followed them and was so engrossed with this task that I didn't realise I had reached the end of the path, a bamboo fence bordering the plot. Next to it were two small heaps: one of broken ceramic waste, the other intact bowls. Why would Matsumoto-san have discarded these bowls? They were undamaged and striking. I selected two from the heap for my aunt; she would love them. I wondered if this act amounted to theft. I would ask Matsumoto-san, I thought, and with a clearer conscience, I returned to the house.

We did not see Matsumoto-san that morning.

'He's been in the studio since dawn,' Midori-san told S-san later as she served us breakfast in the garden. 'He looked rather grim.'

'Let's keep out of his hair,' S-san said, and at once, we laughed; Matsumoto-san was completely bald. We left the house soon enough and drove to Hakone Shrine at the foot of Mount Hakone, along the shores of Lake Ashi. Except for the large orange torii gate, the shrine itself was hidden deep within the forest. We walked up a path from the gate that led to the steps. 'You go,' S-san said, 'there are over eighty steps, and I am afraid I can't climb so many.' She sat down on a flat boulder under a tree. 'I'll wait for you here. The grounds are expansive, so don't wander too far, or you'll get lost.'

S-san was asleep when I returned, her head resting on the trunk of a tree. The sound of water against the shore was musical, lulling. I climbed down some more steps, sat down, and looked up at the torii gate.

'I knew there was a connection between us, other than through your uncle,' I heard her from behind me. 'This torii.'

I turned around to look at her.

'Did you know that the word torii comes from the Indian torana, and its design originated from the gates of the Sanchi monastery? And did you know that Baizaiten, the Japanese goddess, was derived from the Indian deity Saraswati? Some Buddhist temples and Shinto shrines have halls dedicated to her. She is the goddess of everything: water, time, language, music, knowledge.' She stepped down to me, and as I stood up, she held me in her arms.

We drove to Kijitei Hoeiso, a traditional ryokan surrounded by mountains and lush trees. It had an open-air pond fed by a hot spring. S-san knew the owner who gave us a room for the afternoon. 'Let's dip in the water before lunch,' S-san said, 'the sulphur water is good for the skin.' I hesitated. 'Oh, don't be so shy,' S-san said, laughing, 'I am like your mother.' Afterwards, we were served a traditional lunch of soup, pheasant broth, poached fish in soy sauce, and assorted vegetables. I had eaten pheasant before, in a curry. Where? When? My aunt cooked only vegetarian food, and to my knowledge my uncle had never made pheasant. I asked S-san about my aunt. 'I am sure she misses you,' she replied. 'She must be lonely. I know how that feels, and you know how that feels—perhaps you should return home for a while.'

When we returned in the early evening, Matsumoto-san was still in his studio. It was a long dark shed, one end of which opened into a garden that cast pencil-thin shadows of the trellis above. A long stone slab ran the entire length of the room, supported by brick piers. Arranged on it were the most exquisite works of clay art: muted colours, subtle textures, delicate patterns. Matsumoto-san, in a black-brown yukata, was at the wheel, giving form to a lump of clay. He looked up at us but didn't speak. S-san pulled up two stools so that we could sit and watch him work.

'What colours do you like?' he asked me abruptly.

I replied instinctively, 'Childhood colours. The deep-orange of saffron petals, the parrot-green meadows of the mountains, and the sunshine-yellow of mustard flowers.'

'Ah! Vibrant Indian colours. Sometimes I wonder whether Buddhism came from India. Do you know about wabi and sabi?' Not waiting for my reply—he continued, 'Wabi-sabi are the moods of poverty. Sakura-san told me that you are studying photography; they must teach you only the tools and techniques and not the history of art. Let me start at the beginning.' He spoke in English now, 'Listen carefully—

'—Buddhism came to Japan during the beginning of the Middle Ages. At that time, aristocrats controlled the whole country and had no private army; they believed in Buddhism, and the appreciation of beauty was more important to them than military might. They were influenced by the Buddhist concept of mujō—the idea of nothingness: that all things are born, grow, and eventually die, only to begin all over again, an endless cycle. Out of this concept grew the idea of mono-no-aware. It was a period for the art-and-craft of words: literature, poetry, and so on. Mono-no means—of things or events; and aware is, quite simply, the ah, and oh, we express when we find something delightful, startling, or sad and sorrowful. Mono-no-aware is the beautiful sadness of the passing of lives, moments, or things like the autumn leaves that fall or the moon that wanes, the passing seasons, or when a lover leaves. Flowers are beautiful only because they die. Think of it: the cherry blossoms are no more beautiful than any other flower. Their beauty lies in this sadness; they don't last very long. Literature, poetry, song all use mono-no-aware to transform feelings into words.

'A country, however, cannot be led by a group of aristocrats who indulged solely in the beauty and grace of things. Soon, regional military leaders, the samurai, started to threaten these aristocrats. The country came to be ruled by both the Shōgun—the head of the samurai—and the Emperor—the head of the aristocrats. There was conflict amongst them, constant warfare that led to unrest, and the people invariably suffered. It was similar to the end of the Dark Ages in Europe. Many artists abandoned their depressing social lives and became hermits in order to pursue beauty in nature. It was the beginning of the Zen form of Buddhism, whose main tenet was on meditation, to get away from the sorrows of the world, to free oneself. It prescribed stoic conduct over intelligence to pursue truth. Tsurezure is a word used to describe a situation in which you don't have anything in particular to do, to be in a vacant state of mind. Many indulged in the practice of doing nothing, simply being. Zen took the concept of mujō to another level, and art reached a higher level of abstraction, objects were sieved to their purest elements; definitions and meanings were peeled away.

'Then came a period of natural disasters, pandemics, and famine. The population had grown, and it required adequate economic systems, extended networks for goods, and money.

The Shōgun boosted the economy by pushing international trade with China. Now there were wealthy merchants who invested their new-found wealth in the arts and entertainment, especially tea parties, which gave birth to the essence of wabi-sabi: an aesthetics of simple, undecorated, and subtle beauty. It was the beginning of a renaissance.

'Wabi from wabu means to feel disappointed, distressed, or abandoned and lonely. Sabi or sabu means to degrade, decay or rust. Imperfection and a sense of loss *is* wabi-sabi. The culture of mujō primarily resided in literature, poems, but in wabi-sabi, the forms of art shifted to the non-textual: the Zen rock garden, Noh theatre, ikebana, ink painting, and the tea ceremony. None of these relied on text to convey their beauty. A rock surrounded by circles of combed sand is nature frozen. Does it not appear to be alone? Does it not accentuate the loneliness within you?'

The browns of his yukata had slipped into the dimness of the oncoming darkness. Outside, the sky was a Prussian-blue, and I could hear the swishing of the leaves. He looked at me and smiled, 'A solitary rock in the grass surrounded by wildflowers *is* sabu. It is pure art.'

He stood up and wiped his hands on a rag and walked to the long table and carefully selected a bowl—moss green with specks of saffron, orange, and yellow on it—and offered it to me. 'This is for you. Inhale the idea of wabi-sabi, capture your loneliness, and use it in your photography.'

I remembered the two bowls I had picked up that morning and told Matsumoto-san about them. He shrugged his shoulders, 'You should throw them away. They are over a year old.' He walked me towards the door of the shed. 'According to the book of yin and yang, at the beginning of creation, there was only chaos,' he said, 'there was no form for humans, trees, grasses, animals. Because of the yin-yang energy and the hot fires surrounding them, things obtained temporary shapes and forms, and people obtained their souls. After nearly one hundred years, things like utensils, tools, instruments, furniture, and other such inanimate objects obtained spirits; they are called tsukumogami. They are invisible, vengeful spectres. Some become bad people; others become harmful demons and beasts. If the object has been mistreated, they can cause havoc. This is why you have to be careful when you keep or buy old things—their demons could release their wrath on you.'

'So, you believe in superstitions?'

'They are fun, like manga. There's nothing wrong with believing in them so long as they don't harm others or us. After all, superstitions are just different ways of understanding or explaining the mysterious things and occurrences that surround us. They arise from old belief systems that have been passed from person to person through stories and tales about spirits, demons, and such. Superstitions show the creativity of people, their imagination and inventiveness, and the changes in culture. Every period in history has its own storehouse of whimsical fables, and now we have what are called urban legends. They are all important: they tell us about ourselves, our strengths, our weaknesses, our fears. Remember, to move forward in life, you need to do but two things: believe and dream.' He yawned loud and long. 'Good night, I am going to bed now. Midori-san has left some dinner in the kitchen for you.'

After dinner, S-san and I sat on the back veranda. There was no moon that night and no breeze—everything was still. We spoke no words, and our minds were vacant, tsurezure-ing. S-san reached out and caressed my hand; it was a simple gesture, without need for words.

Sarmoli, 2004

My aunt gathered me in her arms and pressed me to her chest. After an early dinner, which consisted of all my favourite things, I asked her why she had been so disheartened. I knew what she would say—she was lonely, and I was far away, she missed me and wanted me to find a husband and settle down—and I knew what I would say. So, I was surprised when she took my hand and led me to the terrace. 'Look,' she said, 'it's not good—the desert rose is dead.'

The tree was empty of flowers and leaves, and its bare branches reminded me of another tree, a lofty chinar, under the shade of which I'd spent many afternoons. Through the year, the leaves fell, and after the winter, no leaves remained. 'Its heart has rotted,' my mother told me.

I found a number of brown envelopes in the drawer of my desk that night; many of them were from Mohan, but some were from Malli. I tore open the most recent one from her. It had an address—Sarmoli, Munsiari, Uttarakhand—a phone number, and a note with only one word, *Come*. I made a decision, and the very next morning, I told my aunt I was going to Munsiari.

'You've just come home, and you want to leave already?' she said irately.

'It's called Little Kashmir,' my uncle said. 'It's a beautiful village in the Himalayas; I went there when I was in college. You should go.'

'Why do you want to go there anyway?' my aunt asked. When I told her about Malli, she retorted, 'You want to go all that way to see a servant girl?'

My uncle tweaked his nose with his fingers. 'Why don't you go with her?' he said to my aunt. 'You've never been anywhere except Bangalore.'

My aunt tweaked her nose back at him. After some minutes, she turned to me, 'So what are you waiting for, eh? Call Malli.'

I called the number Malli had provided. It belonged to a homestay, and the woman who answered said that Malli had not yet come but that she could keep a room for us. I left a message for Malli with her. My aunt stood close to me, an eager look in her eyes. 'It's a homestay's phone number,' I told her, 'and Malli isn't there yet.'

'Oh, she must work there,' my aunt said.

A week later, we were on a train to Kathgodam. I booked a taxi to take us to Munsiari, and then on to Sarmoli—it took us twelve hours to get there. As soon as Malli saw the taxi pull up, she hobbled over to me and gathered me in her arms, laughing with her head tilted back, sunshine in her eyes. Two small children stood watching. My aunt went to the girls with the bags of savouries and sweets she had brought for them. I could hear her ask them their names; *Mogra*, *Jui*, they replied. Just as Malli was, they were other names for Jasmine.

A woman rushed towards my aunt, and when she was closer, I recognised her; it was Saroja. 'My mother came to join me after Patti left Bangalore,' Malli said. 'She lives here now and looks after the children—I am rather busy, you know,' she laughed. 'I have so much to do.' She was rounder now, and her plumpness was not just of flesh but also happiness.

The homestay was built from mud and stone and featured a mosaic of broken tiles pasted on the front wall. Within, the courtyard—filled with flowering trees—was open to the sky. Beyond the two sleeping rooms with beds on the floor, was the kitchen and a rear veranda. Some of the walls were patterned with trees made of broken tiles. Malli said excitedly, 'Ramsingh, my husband, is a contractor of sorts and works in Munsiari—he also runs a taxi service. He got me the broken tiles.'

She had aptly called the homestay, Sapna—*dream*. Malli lived in a house just downhill, an exact copy of Sapna. Her dream was no longer a dream; it had rooted itself into the earth. I was home, though a different sort of home, a home without boundaries, without time, a heart-home where two people resided, Malli and me.

We woke before dawn to view the morning light over Panchachuli—the five peaks of the Himalayan range. Malli spoke in a hush, 'It's beautiful because it changes all the time. I sit here every morning, close my eyes and discard all I can see until there is nothing left, then I open my eyes and fill the empty space and see each thing anew, one by one.'

I closed my eyes, then slowly opened them. The light cut the mountain into sections that seemed to appear and disappear, connect, and then separate again. I *could* see more than I could see. There were thick clouds and translucent clouds, voluminous, soft clouds, and innumerable shards reaching out beyond the peaks. These clouds suggested the itinerant quirk of nature. The rays of the sun, steadily shining through, now lay on the apricot tree in the distance. A lemon tree, closer still, trembled ponderously in the mist. The law of proximity and distance I had learnt at photography school became momentarily obsolescent. Everything before me fitted perfectly, like the yellow dress my mother had stitched meticulously to measure. That memory flitted away as a wild kite swooped through the valley and up over the old teak forest. I held my camera up to capture the scene but quickly changed my mind. I didn't want the lens to come between me and what I saw. Mujō, mono-no-aware, wabi-sabi, were all unfitting here: they trapped beauty as a menagerie of sorts, and their denotations confused me. The loveliness here was free. I breathed long and hard and filled myself with it. The morning air smelled of flowers.

I started to say something, and at once, Malli put a finger to her lips. 'Hum, or sigh, but no words.' Her voice was a faint whisper and sounded more like the sighing of leaves on the nearby willow tree. Many minutes passed until she spoke again. 'If we didn't have words, would we speak? Yes, we need words to talk to one another, but really, there are too many words. Why do we need so many to describe beauty, love, grief, happiness? All we need is an *ah* for surprise and an *oh* for sorrow. Love is mysterious. It should be felt, not described. The many words and their meanings have muddled us, and our minds and hearts have become tangled with them. We have forgotten the simple things.' I heard a sound from above. 'Look, look,' Malli pointed to a branch, 'it's a kathaphodava.' It was a woodpecker, its head orange-red like a gulmohar flower. 'Ramsingh told me that the woodpecker has a very long tongue—as long as the bird itself—to dig deep into the wood to catch insects. It curls its tongue around its neck like a scarf.'

'Where did you meet Ramsingh?'

'His brother is a contractor in Bangalore, and when his business grew, he called his two brothers to help him. They were building a farmhouse in Mohan's father's mango orchard.'

'You met him there?'

'I met him at Meena-ma's house. She had made potato bondas for me, and Ramsingh had been sent by Mohan's father to do some repairs at her house. He told me about his village and the Himalayas, and I knew at once I had to marry him. It was love at second-sight.'

'Second-sight?'

'My first love was always the Himalayas.' She clasped her hands and smiled. 'Meena-ma helped me run away with Ramsingh. I hid in her house for two weeks until he got the train tickets. She gave me food for the journey—and her blessings—and her husband gave me some money. They were leaving for Chicago in a few weeks, and she had given me her son's address. When I wrote to her some months later, she told me her husband had died a week after I left for the mountains, and soon after the funeral, she had left for Chicago with their son. She writes to me regularly now—she's got a good job in a school there, and she's happy; her Gods had listened to her prayers. A while ago, she phoned me and said she would try and come here—"Lord Shiva resides in those mountains," she told me. Here, she would be closer to God.'

Later in the day, whilst Malli and I sat beneath the shade of the big deodar tree, Ramsingh drove my aunt down to Munsiari. Mogra was chasing a butterfly, and Jui was laying on the grass following the toils of a little bug. 'Do they go to school?' I asked.

Malli shook her head. 'Why do we need schools to teach us to live? In the end, that's all there is to life, is it not? Look at the birds, bugs, the butterflies, do they go to school? They do what they have to do, what they are meant to do. They do it not from the heart or the mind but from something deeper within. They don't think, reason, worry, or wonder. They live, they die, and in between, they survive.'

I couldn't argue with her; all that she said contained a flawless rudimentary logic. Instead, I said, 'I'm so happy for you, Malli. You wanted to live close to the Himalayas, you do. You wanted to build your own house, you have. You wished for two girls, and here they are. All your dreams have come true.'

'Yes, but there's a trick to it,' she giggled. 'You have to dream small—' she pointed to the pearls of sunlight filtering through the leaves '—then string all your small dreams like beads in a necklace. The important thing is to know how to begin and when to stop. And never have hope; hope destroys the dreams' spirit. Just let them be, and they will bloom.' She clutched my hand excitedly. 'You know what I'm going to do now: I have taken a loan, and I'm going to build another homestay, and then I'm going to take up potato farming, and then I'm going to build a farm for butterflies, and then I'm going to make wildflower honey.' She sighed, then said, 'I'm going to have to live a very long time.'

In the evening, whilst Malli and Saroja were busy in the kitchen, and my aunt had not yet returned, I went for a stroll along the mountain path. I tried to see everything through Malli's eyes: without words, definitions, categories, analysis, or reasoning. I could never be like her, I thought. She sieved everything to their most basic elements. Living life with such pragmatic simplicity needed courage, and I didn't think I had much of that. I looked up at the peaks. Just like me, alone, I thought. I raised my head and called out my name, and the mountains bellowed it back to me. I was not alone.

It was a long walk, and it was almost dusk when I'd traced my way back. That night, under the moon, the same moon as on all those other nights, the meaning of things seemed to change entirely.

During those five days I spent with Malli, time had no check or limit: day slipped effortlessly into evening, and the sun, moon, stars, even the wind, the birds, and butterflies, all moved in an abiding rhythm. I cherished the idea of tsurezure even more now.

My aunt, though, was busy, and Ramsingh took her to Munsiari every day. When I asked her what she had been doing, she was secretive, but on our last night there, she confided in me. 'I went to a honey farm. I went to a flower orchard. I went to meet an estate agent and saw some properties. I saved all the money I received from the sale of Tatha's house, and I want to move here with your uncle. I want to be close to the mountains, closer to the sky, flowers all around and make honey as sweet as heaven. Most of all, I want to grow a tall desert rose.'

Reshwari, 2004

It was a clear day, and the bushes on either side of the road trembled in the crisp wind. The shadows from the trees moved this way and that, and the stunning green meadows and dense forests of pine and fir climbed the slopes of the hills. The taxi drove past fruit orchards, apple, cherry, peach, apricot. 'Lolab valley is known as the fruit bowl of Kashmir,' my uncle said. He had come to Srinagar to attend a trade meeting, and I had gone with him, and we were now on our way to Reshwari, a small village close to the border.

We stopped to have namkeen chai. I picked walnuts that had fallen from the tree, and my uncle bought three bunches of wildflowers from an elderly woman whose skin was creased and crinkled. 'In half an hour, we will reach Reshwari,' my uncle said, 'and then we have to go a little further to the most beautiful village along the Marwar River.'

The village was small, its houses nestled amidst pine trees on the slope; some of them merely ruins. It started to drizzle when we reached the top of the hill. From there, I could see the desiccated banks of the river gradually dampening. Further along, the market street ran parallel to the riverbank; it was rather large for so small a village. My uncle told me it had been the central market for a number of villages in the surrounding area. We walked on in the rain, finally stopping in front of an old house. It was mildewed and smelled bitter and stale. My uncle laid a bunch of flowers on the doorstep.

On impulse, I ran along the side of the house to the back, and there it was, the green window that wouldn't shut. I could remember the scene vividly: Tasneem, Arun, and I scrambling inside through that window. We would spend many afternoons sharing old ghost stories or making up new ones. One afternoon Arun told us a particularly ghastly story and Tasneem had cried with fear.

'It's only a story, Tasneem,' Arun said. 'Don't cry.'

'I'm not crying because of that,' she said. 'Baba says we have to move to Pakistan.'

I walked back to the front of the house. My uncle was sitting on the steps, his head held in his hands. A stray ray of sunlight was dancing in his hair—it shone golden. He looked up at me, and I sat beside him. 'Arun told us this house was haunted,' I said.

'It was abandoned. The Muslim family who had lived here moved to Pakistan,' my uncle said. 'We used to live in a village similar to this along the border. I was twelve. In those days, I was used to the crackle of fire, the sound of dragging footsteps, rattling windowpanes, screams in the middle of the night. I can still remember burning houses, the smell of burnt bodies. People slept on their feet, leaning against walls, worried and scared that they would soon be uprooted, transplanted to another place. Hindu families started moving from the village. We moved to this house. My father never got over the grief of leaving his village. He was wealthy and owned a lot of land, and he had lost everything. He was miserable and passed away six months later.'

He continued, 'One day, two families—also from our village—came here with their belongings, not to visit but to stay. And each subsequent day brought yet more people. They looked tired. Not of the long journey or the suffering of such a journey, but something else entirely, their eyes seemed afraid, haunted. My mother turned our inner courtyard into a community kitchen. From the terrace, we watched pyramids of fire and thick black smoke curling into the sunlit sky. I saw groups of people carrying small bundles of luggage, and when I asked my mother about them, she said, "They're fugees, Hindus from Pakistan, fugees." She meant refugees. The next day, some of our neighbours in the village left their houses in the middle of the night. When I asked my mother why they had left, she said only, "They're islims." She meant Muslims.'

'Where is your mother?'

'She's gone. An accident,' is all he said. 'After that, I moved to Bombay.'

I remembered what Meena-ma's husband had said: that the country had gone mad.

We walked down the other side of the hill. My uncle stopped at a house blackened with soot and consumed by creepers. He laid the other bunch of flowers at its unhinged door. I watched as a colony of ants transported a grasshopper into a crack on the floor. I stooped down to rescue it then realised it was already dead, though its green colour remained vibrant. I turned away and looked up at the tall chinar tree nestled beside the gate, bereft of leaves; the apple tree up the hill was full of fruit.

'Whose house is this?' I asked, but my uncle didn't reply, only sighed. The old willow tree seemed to sigh with him, and below us, the waters of the Marwar tinkled ceaselessly. A bird tumbled in the wind, drifting on taut wings. I remembered the wild pigeons cooing through the afternoon, the bats cheeping peevishly at night. I remembered the cacophony of crows when the stars swelled into the gentle dawn light that loomed across the night sky. I remembered the willow tree, the ants and bugs that scurried across its branches. The wind was different here—it was sharp and cold but moist, expansive, with arms to hold me. It had banged against the shutters, and the willow tree had groaned against the window. It could get fierce sometimes, the wind, but now, as it touched my skin, I remembered my mother's saree on the clothesline billowing in the breeze, and with a slap, it fluttered inside out. I had loved that particular saree, the colour of ice. In the pit of my stomach, I felt a deep sadness knotted tight, it was sour, and it stung my eyes.

My uncle grasped my hand, and we walked down another path to a tar road that lead to the market. A rickety truck carrying apples passed us, and I heard the sound of shoes as a mother, and her daughter, ran past us. She must have been five or six. I remembered my mother walking me to the market; she would buy me cotton candy, soft, sweet, pink.

The rain had stopped, and my uncle rested at a spot near the bus stop under a walnut tree with thick red-and-white stripes painted on its trunk. I had a vague memory of this place, a faded watercolour drawing. I remembered the bus driver who chewed betel leaf who would stop here, spit the paan juice at the tree, which had measles of red spots on its bark. There, next to a boulder at the side of the road, my uncle set down the remaining flowers.

'What's here?' I asked.

'Here is a moment I can never forget,' my uncle said. He looked up at the chinar tree. 'I planted this twenty years ago,' he said, 'it was just a sapling then. Look how tall it has grown.' He sat beneath it and closed his eyes.

I walked down the road towards the market. There were grocery and vegetable shops, butchers, tanners, and utility stores. Off the street, in the shadowy alleys, were rows of shacks with piles strewn around: newspaper, cardboard boxes, glass bottles, and soot and grease stuck to everything. Even though it was still light, it was gloomy in these alleys. Houses with drowsy windows let in the breeze from the chinar trees.

I walked back to the wooden bridge that straddled the small canal of water. I watched a spider weaving one arc at a time, moving to and fro, to and fro. Now and then, it seemed to tremble, a string of dribble dropped from its mouth, and it tumbled from its web. I looked away. Further down, I saw a little girl crouched in the ditch; she was six years old. I remembered her. I had constructed borders in my mind to prevent her memories from tormenting me, but they had remained in the deep womb of my mind, had never really left, and when I looked deep into her eyes, I could see flecks of what she had seen all those years ago.

Cheru, the epileptic, had had a fit in front of the temple. Gooru, the drunk milkman, wakes from his torpor, considers the frantic crowd outside the mosque, sucks a mouthful of blackened air, and falls back to sleep. An old woman trips over a plant with purple flowers potted in an old rusted tin of baby milk powder. She picks it up, and the baby's face smiles back at her. She kisses it, and then, cradling the tin on her hip—as though it were her child—she continues on down the road. Hers is a familiar face, a known face, a remembered face. Those brown eyes and the nose, one that begins and ends too rapidly, a broad, flower-like snout. What was her name? Her hand goes up to her mouth, and she screams. I can see the hollow of her throat, the fresh pink.

My heart misses a beat, and I press my hand to my chest as if to clutch the beat in my fist. My fingers sigh open, and I release the throb into the air. Standing on the bridge, I recall scene after scene, as in a corridor of mirrors, and moment by moment, they ricochet within me. I am drenched by old images as they force their way out of the bulwarks of my mind. There was an uncanny melodrama to these unfolding images as though I were in a cinema watching a film unroll. But I wanted to remember, needed to. I was consumed by a notion which, until then, had never once occurred to me: if I could persevere with these memories, I would not be susceptible to anything, so I nudged my memory on.

It is Saturday, market day. My uncle is with us. My mother asks Arun and me to get some things from the market. We walk down the hill. We are in the middle of the market street. We pass the mosque. It is painted a brilliant green and stands beside the Devi temple, its very own twin. Tube lights hang from metal brackets, and the loudspeaker atop the dome spurts: *La ilaha illallah*. Around the same time, the bells in the Devi temple clang, and devotees chant in one seamless voice. Incense fumes rise into the air dousing the sky above with the scent of belief. Faith is strong here; this is not unusual. At times of festivals and marriage, they feast together, both Hindus and Muslims, but they love their gods separately. Anxiously. Painstakingly. They do not forget their differences, but they choose to endure. The option is important, and it is clear. The Muslim girl would walk the Hindu child to school, hand in hand. The Hindu girl would tie a rakhi on a Muslim boy's wrist, claiming him as her chosen brother. This is not unfamiliar. Over the years, the village by the river has soaked up the stories of the land, its different peoples, their good deeds, their misdeeds.

A large crowd has gathered in the market. They shout out their protests, heads raised, arms above them. This is not uncommon, either, and happens from time to time. From the radio, I hear a popular song. I hear the wind in the trees, softly at first, then more menacingly. Then I hear angry voices. A mob of men rush into the street, their faces distended with anger. They set a shop on fire and then another. 'Run,' a shopkeeper yells at us. Arun clutches my hand, and we run past the temple, past the mosque, past the burning shops. We collide with Rani-ma, the old woman with the baby milk powder tin; she smells of stale fruit. We continue on. We stop beneath a tree at the edge of the market; the sky is crocheted with rising smoke, billowing into the clouds. I see shops ablaze and close my eyes, but I can still hear the sound of fire. The street has a smell I am unused to, and it is crowded with people who are packed so closely that I can smell their fear-sweat, which smells like everything else does, of burnt fish. An explosion slashes the clouds, and the sky is flush with fire. The windows of nearby houses fly open like book pages in a wild wind, and several heads peep out. People run from doors, crash into each other, beat on each other with their fists. They scream as gunshots rip the air. As the birthmark on his face reddens, and in a voice gone shrill with fear, Arun screams, 'Run, run, run.' And so I run. In the commotion, I let go of his hand. I can see him running across the wooden bridge and down the road without me. Nervous in my knees, I climb into the ditch beneath the bridge and hide. I shut my eyes tight, and only when the noise has subsided do I open them. The windows of the house across from me are smashed, and the door, I look for the door, but there isn't one. In its place, only the looming darkness. Strewn on the road are wooden fragments, broken glass, photo frames, a hammer, books, a sheet, a saree, a single shoe. I wonder where the other is. I smell fresh blood and another, stranger smell, burning, a smell of burnt rubber, of burnt skin, and hair. I see Rani-ma screaming, running down the street, the flowering plant at her hip. A man pushes against her with the butt of his gun, and the plant crashes to the floor. 'My child, mera beta,' Rani-ma seizes the tin, kisses the baby's face, then scrambles to the ditch. Rivers of wrinkles run across her face. Her eyes are as empty as the doorway. She covers herself with her saree, crouches next to me, and for a split second, there is an overwhelming silence. Everything is suspended, and then I hear Arun calling my name, despair in his voice. He is running back towards the bridge. I hear a gunshot and see him stumble and then fall. I shriek. I run to him. I'm not sure if he's dead. His eyes remain open, are as cold as a pair of brooches made from steel. Fear fills the void, not huge like a chasm, but tiny. His nostrils and lips twitch as the cold wind slashes his face, and a small trail of blood escapes his mouth. He shudders and shuts his eyes. He is dead. I am certain now. Rani-ma rushes to me, clutches my hand, and together we clamber through the fields. Nearer home, whilst people crowd on the road, pyramids of fire rise high into the night sky. The men are shouting, the children and women crying. Tersely, a woman laughs. It is madness: the shouting, the crying, the shrill laughter. 'Ma, Papa,' I cry out, but no one responds.

Standing on the old wooden bridge, I had remembered. I climbed down into the ditch where the little girl had hidden,

I sat against the trunk of a tree, and with my eyes shut, I cried silently. I don't know how long I sat there, though it seemed an eternity, and after which there was only me.

'What are you doing there?' I heard my uncle say. 'We should leave now. The taxi's waiting, and it's a long way back to Srinagar.'

It was late when we reached our hotel. I kept the lights on that night. I tried to sleep, but shadows like the wings of a giant moth folded over me each time I shut my eyes. I had sealed my memories away carefully, frozen them for so many years, but now, my mind flicked through them as my fingers would the pages of a book. I shut my eyes and hoarded away the memories of the little girl.

Tokyo, 2004

It was sultry for the time of year. The nanten bushes were drenched, and the evening light that reflected off the raindrops on the leaves looked like brilliant baubles. S-san walked into the veranda with two glasses of beer and set them on the table. 'It's been so hot since you went away,' she said, wiping the back of her neck with a handkerchief. She sat down and took a large gulp of the cold beer. 'Now, tell me, how are your aunt and uncle? Tell me about your trip.'

I told her about Sarmoli and Malli, about the lost village in the Lolab Valley. I told her about the house on the hill, about the boulder on the road where my uncle had offered flowers, and about how desolate he had been.

S-san was lost in thought. With a deep sigh, she said, 'We were quite alike, your uncle and me. He laughed a lot, though it was only a façade; the deep sadness and lingering loneliness consumed him. I haven't talked about it since he told me, but your uncle never got over the death of his son. Imagine finding your son's body on the road the day after he was shot. It's very sad.' She sighed. 'After Arun died, he was broken, yet he smiled, always.'

S-san stared at the bamboo bushes. 'The only person I ever really loved was your uncle, but he was already married. It was not to be. We have been good friends for a long time now.' She held my hands in hers as her eyes turned dewy. 'And now, through you, there is another connection between us, which makes me very happy.'

I stared blankly at her. I caught a glimpse of the bushes beyond her dripping wet, and the tears I'd been holding inside began to fall.

I met Ryu a few days later. I was glad to see him, and he to see me. We had donburi for lunch at a restaurant near Hongō station, and he asked if I had taken any interesting photos. 'I didn't take any,' I said. 'The lens couldn't capture the things I saw and felt.'

He laughed, 'Never mind, we still have more than enough time to complete the assignment.'

I didn't see Ryu the next day. As usual, I waited for him in front of the bank. I wondered if I should call him, then decided against it. He never called me when I was late, and once, when he hadn't turned up, and I *had* called him, he had asked me not to call again and to not wait for him. 'If I am not there on time, it means I can't make it,' he said curtly. 'There's always some trouble at home, things I can't explain, things I don't need to.' I reasoned something urgent must have come up.

I was worried about Ryu, and as the days passed, I became even more anxious about the course work, realising I would have to complete it alone. Determined but panicked, I walked the streets. I assumed street photography would be easy, and my pictures seemed adequate, but I wasn't sure. Some of my distress dissipated when Akiko called. 'Good, you're back,' she said. She invited me to her photo exhibition at the Saké Art House. 'I think you'll like it.'

I left early with my camera. On the side street leading to Asakusa Temple, I took pictures of the criss-crossed wires above. They were so dense and interlaced that all I could see was an uneven patchwork sky. Closer to the temple, I saw through the tangle of wires, two women dressed in bright orange kimono. I captured them on the screen.

I turned onto the main street and walked to the bar; it was crowded, and Akiko was giving an interview. When she had finished, she walked up to me and kissed me on both cheeks. I could smell her scent, which had a hint of fresh lemons. I couldn't help smiling; she had a plaster across her nose. 'Accident,' she said. I didn't believe her, though I did notice another plaster on her elbow and thought, perhaps, what she had said was true.

I looked at the photos on the wall, stunning, crisp, urban. Each with a story about the things left behind on the street: an umbrella, a hat, a glove, white and blue plastic bags strewn about, and the backs of people as they walk away.

'It started as a photo for a music album, *Walk Away*. I shot a whole series after that,' Akiko said.

After a round of beer, I showed her my pictures. 'Beautiful,' she said. I felt relieved. 'But too pretty,' she shook her head. 'It's like the difference between crisp prose and tender poetry. Both are equally good, but I prefer prose in particular: the raw beauty of things.' I sulked, and she laughed. 'Don't be upset,' she said, 'street photography is the most challenging of all; it keeps changing, and you need to be quick to respond. Getting a good image of an ordinary street takes a fraction of a second —if you miss the moment, it is gone forever.' She looked at the photos again. 'Each one of your photos is good, but there is nothing connecting them. You must tell a story through your pictures about the people in them, about chance encounters and random incidents, so that the viewer can pause and pose questions in their mind as they interact with them. It could be a single story or a collection of short stories.' She twitched her nose. 'Besides, you need to record street life from your own unique perspective—this becomes your personal style. Watch people and how the light falls on them, the shadows, and how they relate to their surroundings. Set the stage: choose a background carefully and wait for an interesting character to enter the frame.'

'I don't know if I can do this.'

'You'll be fine,' she smiled. 'Roam the streets. Examine what you see. Think of a working title for your photo story, then take photos to fit the title. Remember, the photos must speak. They shouldn't need words to describe them.' She glanced through the photos I had taken an hour ago. 'These are very good.' She twitched her nose again, pulled off the plaster. 'This really tickles.'

I walked the streets of Harajuku, Shibuya, and Shinjuku over the next few days. I had a title for the series: *Wired*, the street, buildings, people, all seen through the overhead wires. They were not pretty pictures, but they were convincing, they were real.

I was on Hongō Street one morning when I saw Ryu by the tree outside of the bank. He was dressed in a formal suit and not his usual baggy jeans and T-shirt. He saw me cross the road and tried to hide behind the tree. When I reached him, he looked down and quietly said, 'Sorry, I didn't come all these days. My father had a heart attack. We only brought him home from the hospital last night.'

'I'm so sorry,' I said. 'Is he okay?'

'It was a mild attack,' he said. 'He's okay but weak.' He took a long breath. 'I called the bank and asked for my old job back; I need the money and won't be continuing the class. My mother is terribly sad for me. "You have to do what you have to do when you have to it," she said.'

His voice trembled, and he sounded tearful, but when he looked back up at me, his eyes were blank, bereft of any tears; his eyes, so deep and intense, had misplaced their oku.

Kyoto, 2006

I was in Kyoto to spend some time with Ojiisan and Obaasan. They had recently moved to their new house, and Ojiisan had become gaunt, listless—the light had gone from his eyes. He reminisced about his old house as though he had lost a long-standing, dependable friend. I had, too; I didn't know what to make of their new house.

All I could see from the street was a large concrete wall with a small, *Alice in Wonderland*-esque, red door. On the other side, though, the house was like a crystalline-rock cut open: tall steel columns supported the roof made entirely from treated glass. The exterior walls were made of sandwiched, glass panels and the gaps between were filled with glass beads —with the tap of a switch, water trickled between them, making patterns as the light filtered through. Seen through the glass, the trees outside were a greenish blur. The rooms on either side were partially concealed beneath the earth, covered with undulating turf. The main focus, sculpture-like, was the free-standing red staircase leading to Ojiisan's new atelier. Slightly askew, this atelier faced the sky so that he could experience the splendour of each new dawn and dusk.

Many people came to see the house: friends, neighbours, reporters, and photographers. Yasunari arrived with the crew from a local television channel and talked to them about the new house. Obaasan didn't say much. Ojiisan appeared unruffled at first, at least on the surface; perhaps it was his way of preserving his dignity. But he failed to hold back for too long. 'I feel like a carp trapped in a glass aquarium,' he said to one of the reporters. 'I feel naked, and there's too much light,' he said to another. To the cameraman of the television channel, he said, 'So many trees around, but I can hardly see them through the fixed glass, and there aren't any windows. There's only a small door to get into the garden. I feel abandoned on an island with nowhere to go.' It was his first television interview.

Yasunari was saddened by Ojiisan's remarks. They had a heated argument, and Yasunari decided to leave the house.

After that, something changed with Ojiisan and soon after Yasunari had returned to Tokyo, Ojiisan stepped out of his room with a suitcase. 'I can't live here,' he said, 'I'm leaving.' Despite the light spilling in through the glass, his face was cloaked in darkness.

'Where will you go, Ojiisan?' Obaasan asked, wrinkles gathering around her eyes.

'I will live with the monks at the monastery.' His face looked grim rather than sad. He banged his head violently against the glass wall. 'Let me go,' he shouted, 'let me out.' A lost and hapless jailbird in a glass cage, he beat his hand on the wall repeatedly.

Obaasan tried to console him. 'Lie down and rest awhile. It's all right—it's all right,' she calmed him. 'You will feel better. You will grow stronger. Don't worry, Ojiisan.'

He seemed to have lost his purpose to live.

* * *

It was a stormy night when he died.

The tsuya—*the passing of the night*—was not performed inside the house as it was usually: the house was not designed for death. Ojiisan's corpse was, instead, placed in the garden under the ginkgo tree. Yasunari, his parents, and Hiroo—conspicuous because of his lime green shirt—stood close by. Katayama-san stood at a distance dressed in white.

I watched, tearlessly, as Obaasan lit candles and incense sticks, the fragrant fumes of which baffled the mosquitoes. A sparrow flew from the tree to the glass roof and then dashed back to the tree. Her mind pared, and her hair loose, flying in the wind, Obaasan hugged the ginkgo tree. The old kimono holding her together.

I heard the familiar bell and cry from the street: *Yaki-imo, yaki-imo, yaki-imoooo*. Obaasan turned; 'Ojiisan loves yaki-imo,' she said, and ran past me.

That night, when I could no longer bear the cramped feeling in my chest, I walked out of the room, out of the hall, out of the door, and then down to the end of the street, the end of another street near the woods, until I came to the very end, and I could go no further. It was cold. I sat down beneath a tree and wrapped my body with my arms: my arms and my hair seemed to grow longer, and my eyes seemed to grow wider. Through the trellis of my hair, I looked up at the night sky. I felt the wind retreat, the birds return, and the trees sway from me, and I wished for time to rewind so I could once again be where I was born.

I cried. I cried for Ojiisan and Obaasan, for my mother and father, and for Arun, I wept.

Obaasan talked to the chrysanthemums, the pink-white azalea blossoms, and the shikuramen blooms she kept under the shade of the ginkgo tree. 'They will hate to be inside the glass cage,' she said. 'They will die just like Ojiisan did.' With a sheet of fine tissue paper, she soaked up the dewdrops on the spiderwebs. She talked to the ants that ran up the sticky stems of the flowers. She threw her arms around the ginkgo tree and said to it, 'It's all right now. Don't worry. I know, I know, the storm was strong the night Ojiisan died. I will look after you now, and you will become strong again. It will be all right. It's okay. Trust me.'

It was as though Ojiisan had been her clock; everything she did around the house was timed according to his needs. She no longer fussed about the house arranging the books and old mementos, wiping away fine dust, dislodging cobwebs. She did not fret about what she had to make for breakfast, lunch, or dinner. I cleaned the house, went to the market, washed clothes, answered the phone, talked, cooked, and once, when I gave Obaasan the ginkgo nuts I had roasted, she asked, 'Where did you get these?'

'From the ginkgo tree.'

'Our ginkgo tree? Oh! I didn't see the flowers. I didn't even notice the buds. So the tree is well now—Ojiisan loves ginkgo nuts.' Her face filled with delight. She looked inevitable, as though part of a plot she knew nothing of.

I spoke quietly so as not to upset her. I talked about soft things: the curve of a branch, the twinkling stars. I held out a conch shell—smelling of fish, of the sea, of the sand. I held it to her ear. Her face, reflected in the glass wall of the house, seemed to have lost all sense of joy. I had never seen such lonely eyes.

The next morning I found Obaasan in the kitchen taking old pots and pans down from the shelves. 'I have to throw these out,' she said. 'They have become tsukumogami. They bring misfortune and death.' She made bundles of Ojiisan's things—some old clothes and furnishings—and I helped her cart them to the alley. She sat down, rested her back against the compound wall. 'Now the tsukumogami won't trouble us,' she said. 'Ojiisan didn't believe in tsukumogami. He was stupid, and now he's dead.'

Katayama-san came regularly. His eyebrows were long and curled over his beady eyes. He didn't talk much, but he often smiled. His skin was pale, and I could see his veins through it. He was always dressed in white, and Obaasan cheered up whenever she saw him. 'Don't worry about her,' he said when I told him I would have to leave soon: I had to resume my classes, and my uncle was back in Tokyo. 'You go, I will look after Obaasan.'

Obaasan sat by the pond, and I brought us cups of green tea. I plugged in the repellent device, slipped the blue tablet into its smiling face, and sat down on the wooden plinth beside her. She swirled the water in the glass urn with a stick, pouring the entire bottle of black dye into it. 'The colour of death,' she said, 'a sadder shade of dark—the colour never fades.'

I agreed.

We fell silent. Deep in our own thoughts, the moments flowing along separate paths. 'Death is always a surprise,' Obaasan said. 'We never can know how we are going to die. Even as a young child, I worried about how my parents would die. And when I married, I worried about how my husband would die, my son, me. The thought of death is even more intense than death itself.' She let out a long-held breath. 'People will do anything to be alive, to feel alive, but they should look more closely at death. They should prepare for death long before they are dead.'

She narrowed her eyes, looked out at the darkness of the trees. 'My parents lived in Hiroshima. I had gone to visit them when I was pregnant with Shigeru. It was a Monday morning, the 6th of August 1945. The breeze was cool beneath the ginkgo tree, and the birds were singing. Suddenly I felt something warm on my cheek as if someone had stroked it with a hot towel. I turned back and thought I saw a mirror falling from the sky. Then I heard a roaring sound that shook the entire ground. A huge column of clouds appeared not far from the mountains in the south. It was not an ordinary cloud, though, and seemed to form into a huge mushroom, dark and ominous. Soon the sky darkened. My father rushed into the garden and said he had heard on Radio Tokyo that an American plane had dropped a bomb and that, a hot wind had slammed against the people, had burnt them instantaneously. "When the heatwave reached the ground, it scorched everything to ashes. The city has become an ocean of fire," he said.

'My mother had been visiting her friend not far from where the bomb was dropped; she had left home early. We rushed out into the street but couldn't move; there were so many people. We couldn't do anything except wait anxiously, hour after hour. The next day we went to the city center. We heard the screams of people buried beneath the debris, hurt, abandoned. There were cries of *water, water*. We searched for hours, but we couldn't find my mother or her friend.

'My father persuaded me to return to Kyoto. "For the sake of your child," he pleaded, but I refused to leave him, and we returned to Kyoto two weeks later. Then, at the beginning of September, I received a wrinkled-up postcard. The card read: *I am at the centre on Miyajima*. There was also a rudimentary map of the island inside. The date on the card indicated that many days had passed since she had written it. The next day we left for Miyajima.

'We looked for my mother in the largest room at the center and found her lying facedown. She had shrunk, and when my father lifted the cloth covering her back, I saw the burns. Her eyes were filled with pus, and her flesh had rotted. She died some days later,' Obaasan sighed. Tears were flowing down her cheeks. 'I have never been able to forget the smell of soured blood.'

Her face was now a mask, her mouth closed and eyes bereft. She turned to me. 'You should visit Hiroshima—it is a reminder to us, to all people, of the horrors of death.'

It was quiet except for the occasional sound of the ginkgo nuts as they fell to the ground. Obaasan looked at me and said, 'After the bomb exploded, the fires destroyed all the trees; only the ginkgo trees survived. They are called hibakujumoku—A-bombed trees. You will see them.' She sighed. 'Go and hug a tree for me—please tell me you will?'

'Yes, I will.'

'Promise?'

I replied, squeezing her hand, 'Yes, I promise.'

Tokyo, 2006

We were at a French restaurant in Ginza, Shigeru-san and Keiko-san, S-san, my uncle and me; Keiko-san had booked the table for us. The place was posh and designed in an old French style: high ceilings with decorative mouldings, Rococo-style wall panels, vintage furniture, and gorgeous chandeliers. Keiko-san had recently returned from a trip to Paris. 'I love French food,' she told us, 'so much more than Italian. And this is an expensive place—not everyone can afford it.' She was dressed in a chic black midi with a plunging back and a slit running right up to her thigh, and her hair was coloured a chestnut brown. She leaned towards S-san and said, 'You know, red hair in Paris is passé. This shade of brown, however,' she pointed to her head with her forefinger, 'is in fashion.' She rattled off the names of designer stores she had shopped in. 'I bought a lot.' She laughed; it was a squeal, childish, and nervous. 'My husband is so fretful about it all. I even bought a new car after my return from Paris.'

'Is it brown?' S-san asked.

'Yes,' Keiko-san replied. 'How did you guess?'

'It must match your hair.'

Keiko-san ignored that remark. 'Now, where is Yasunari? He said he was bringing a friend.' She looked at me. 'I think it must be his girlfriend; he told me it was someone special.'

S-san chortled. 'You'll be surprised,' she said.

'I'm not surprised at all,' Keiko-san retorted. 'Yasu-chan is rich and famous. So many girls are after him now.'

Shigeru-san ordered a bottle of French wine.

Keiko-san raised her glass to her lips. 'French wine is so much better than Italian, and—' she abruptly stopped. Her eyes were fixed on the door. Hiroo stood there, dressed in a vibrant-green silk shirt, his arm wrapped around Yasunari's shoulder. They walked to our table.

Hiroo leant towards her. 'Ravi de vous rencontrer madame,' he said and turned and waved a hand to us.

'Thank you, Maman,' Yasunari said, sitting down. Hiroo sat beside him. 'Hiroo loves French food. He brought me here only a week ago when it opened; the food is excellent.'

'I heard it's expensive,' S-san remarked.

'It is but ma chére Maman is paying. Aren't you?' he looked at his mother and beamed.

'Are you an architect?' Shigeru-san asked Hiroo. 'Do you work with Yasunari?'

'I am a stylist,' Hiroo replied. 'Ma chére Maman is a stylist too. She lives in Paris.'

'And your father?' S-san asked.

'He is here, in Tokyo. He is a businessman.'

'So, you live with him?' Keiko-san asked.

'Of course not. Définitivement pas! I live with your son.' Hiroo turned, raised his hand, and called out, 'Serveur, s'il vous plait.'

Yasunari said, 'Hiroo speaks French. I'm learning from him.'

The waiter poured wine into Hiroo and Yasunari's glasses. I heard a distinct clink, then another, and then several more. I looked up at the enormous chandelier; it was swaying to and fro. The clinking sound intensified, and I heard a crash from the kitchen, the sound of dishes tumbling down. A decorative vase fell from the cabinet in front of me. I felt the floor move beneath my feet, and then, with a thud, it shot up and then down again. 'Earthquake. Earthquake,' someone shouted. People scrambled out of the room.

Hiroo stood; his face was ashen. 'Tremblement de terre,' he said. He darted in the direction of the door, and Yasunari ran after him. Keiko-san began to shriek, her arms swinging violently.

S-san leaned towards me and held my hand. 'Don't panic,' she said, 'it will pass.' Oddly enough, a hunger suddenly overcame me; I could feel the void in my stomach.

The tremor lasted only a few minutes, and then everything, everyone, was quiet.

Later, back at S-san's house, my uncle asked me, 'Will you be alright?'

S-san said, 'Don't worry. She can sleep at my house tonight. Why don't you come in for coffee?'

We sat on the back veranda. A fierce breeze pushed through the trees, and the nanten bushes tinkled noisily. All of a sudden, the gust stopped, and I could hear the night birds calling out.

The poodle, curled at S-san's feet, whined.

My uncle sipped his coffee. 'This is good.'

'Honestly, that Keiko-san is something else,' S-san said. 'I wonder how Shigeru-san puts up with her.'

My uncle said, 'You'd be surprised, he likes her that way. He wants a stylish wife he can show off to his friends. She's his pet project. She came from a poor family, was a skinny, small-town girl, long black hair, no make-up, ill-fitting clothes. She worked in an auto dealer's showroom. That's how Shigeru met her—when he went to buy a car. She knows a lot about cars; she loves cars, and he loves her.'

'Relationships are strange,' S-san said.

I remembered what Obaasan had said about relationships, that they faded unless they were fleeting, or founded on selfless love, or better still, a tragedy. I glanced at S-san and then my uncle. There was so much togetherness between them that it was rather tragic they were not together, but their love had possibly sustained because of this. Theirs was a different kind of love, a love that never tired.

I began to hum *Shikuramen No Kaori*. S-san started singing along; she had a mellifluous voice.

Hiroshima, 2006

My uncle and I went on the train to Hiroshima.

At the Peace Memorial Museum, surrounded by noisy school children, I looked at the photographs of the bombing: streets cluttered with debris, scorched bricks, melted asphalt, burnt rubber, atomic dust, bloated buildings, their walls pushing out from the earth, separated, burnt trees, scorched telephone poles and wires, people fleeing, their hair burnt and skin hanging from their faces, flesh-blown limbs. A stray blue bicycle: paint blistered but otherwise intact, its wheels like two spoked eyes, witness to the rush of destruction. Amidst it all were people consoling people. I closed my eyes; I could smell the stink of hate, the scent of love.

I felt Obaasan's pain. 'It's so horrible,' I said. 'So many people died here.'

My uncle's voice was calm. 'People go away all the time. Departing is natural, more natural than birth even. Many births are accidents. Passing away due to old age, disease, hazards like drought, floods, or earthquakes is natural, but this, Kavya, is an aberration.'

I heard my mother whisper, 'I named you Kavya—a poem, the poem of my life.' My mother had stitched me a yellow dress for my birthday, the colour of sunflowers. I was five.

Outside the museum, the ground was carpeted with autumn leaves, some yellow, others still green. The fan-shaped leaves of the ginkgo tree had turned a vibrant shade of gold. Just as Ojiisan had told me they would, the fetid smell of their berries soaked the air.

I hugged the ginkgo tree; I could hear the stories deep within its sap. My sadness remained a lump in my throat. I remembered a dream within a dream, lying beneath an apple tree, sunlight trickling through the leaves, Arun holding my hand.

The past crumbled bit by bit beneath my feet; I had nothing left to hold on to. I had a deep longing for human warmth, so I clutched my uncle's hand. He looked at me, pain in his eyes.

I whispered, 'I'm so sorry your son's gone.'

Kyoto, 2006

I completed my photography course some months later and would soon be leaving for Bombay. Before I left, I went to Kyoto to see Obaasan. I was surprised when I saw her: she wore a trendy skirt, face powder, and a rich lip colour. Her skin was pallid under the make-up, so were her eyes, and her tinted lips were pursed. Her long hair was cut short and coloured a deep mahogany brown. When I remarked that she looked younger and different, she said, 'It's a new beginning.'

I followed her into the house. Yards of indigo-dyed cloth hung in the living space, and there were large vats filled with dye and water and shelves lined with raw, untreated fabric. Two young women were on the floor, folding and stitching cloth. Katayama-san was with them; he waved to me. As always, he was dressed in white.

'My house is now my workshop,' Obaasan explained. 'Katayama-san helped me convert the shed at the back into my bedroom, close to my lovely azaleas.' She looked happy.

That evening we sat in the garden; Obaasan brought cups

of tea. 'So many mosquitoes.' She sat down and looked up at the moon. Besides its light, the only glow came from the electronic mosquito repellent device.

'I'm no different,' she said. 'All this is only cosmetic; I'm the same—we remain the same. Yasunari and young people like him are exactly like the young people of the past. Only the clothes, the houses, the stuff they use, and the ways in which they do things are different. People's minds are the same. They need to love, they need to hate, and everything they do is only a means to achieve these basic needs of living a life.' Her hair was reddened by the moonlight. 'In the end, everything is the same.'

Everything was indeed the same: the paving stones were still lined with evening mist, the ginkgo tree still swayed in the wind; a sudden breeze ruffled its leaves. The carps in the pond twirled in the moonlight, and a bewildered sparrow flew from the roof to the cherry tree.

The moon shone down on us, and I felt Obaasan clasp my arms and lift me up. And there we stood, holding one another, embracing all that was.

Epilogue

The evening light cuts the five peaks of the Panchachuli mountains into segments of greyer shades of dark. The sky turns red, then orange, and then red-orange as the sun begins to set. I cover my eyes with both my hands. Minutes pass, I look through my fingers, I see the sky: a purple drape sequinned with stars.

In more ways than one, it is a great relief for me to be here. The surrounding hills are resonant with the cry of the cicadas and the majestic dark clouds towering above them. In the darkness, the mountains lose the particulars of their structure. The trees below are steadily veiled by the dusky night. The willow tree nearby is cloaked in a blue haze, and as a cool summer breeze ruffles its leaves, it sighs. A flock of birds spring from its branches, flying into the darkening clouds.

One memory remains—the memory of the sun streaming through the stencil of leaves, and Arun lying beside me on the thick summer grass. Night-time, and we sit under the apple tree watching the stars. My mother comes to us with a bowl of roasted walnuts. She is tall, with long black hair braided into a plait, and she has a mole over her upper lip; I have one too, just smaller, only a dot. Her eyes were brown; I have my father's eyes, the colour of clouds on a rainy day.

I think back on the six years since I returned from Tokyo. A lot had happened in such a short time. Mohan returned from Chicago: he had wanted to stay on, but his mother had compelled him to return to Bangalore, and so he had. We talked often on the phone. He worked for an IT company. 'I am making a lot of money,' he told me. 'I'm happy,' he said, though I knew he was not. He missed Chicago as I missed Tokyo. Our combined discontent became our bond.

I worked for a leading newspaper in Bombay; it was a good job, but I didn't love it. So, in my free time, I compiled photo essays, sent them to a photo agency, and was thrilled when a few of them got published. I took some time off from my job and returned to my childhood village to shoot pictures of it: the river, the desiccated sandbank, empty houses, desolate mountain paths, the wooden bridge, the market street, the alleys, the graveyard, solitary tombs, and the bare chinar. I had a small exhibition of them in Bombay. The reviews were complimentary; the dead chinar tree was everyone's favourite. I sent the pictures to my photo agent but didn't hear from her.

It was during the monsoon of the next year that Mohan came to work in Bombay. He visited often, and my aunt fussed over him; she liked him a lot. My uncle, however, was indifferent and aloof. I asked him about this once, 'Why are you so unfriendly with Mohan?'

'I hope you are not too close to him.' His brow creased with worry.

I laughed. 'Of course not, we're just friends.'

I took Mohan to the Chowpatty beach after the rains. The sand was still damp, so we sat on a wooden bench and ate bhelpuri, and watched the waves heave out from the viscous sea, then recede, over and over again. The palm trees swished in the wind, and gulls flew on damp wings. I watched a baby crab dart across the sand. Mohan's voice was a whisper, as though he didn't want to hear himself say the words, 'We should get married.' I heard the waves withdraw again.

I did feel close to him but had never considered marrying him: there were only fine strings that connected us, we were so unlike one another, and so I didn't know what to say to him. It was rather comic, the more I thought of it. I laughed, not because what he had said was amusing, but because his expression was grave and afraid. 'Not with that face,' I said.

Now, even his smile was solemn. 'I do want to marry you,' he said, 'but my mother will never allow it.'

This remark nettled me. 'Why not? There's nothing wrong with me, is there?'

'It's not that,' he hesitated. 'It's because you're an orphan. Besides, there is the matter of caste.'

I was enraged. 'Let's get married then.'

Mohan returned to his old job, and so, some months after we were married, we moved into his parents' house. I now faced an unfamiliar set of circumstances. I had to change it or learn to deal with it; I opted to change it. 'Let's find a place of our own,' I said to Mohan.

Mohan talked to his mother—she wouldn't hear of it. 'Don't poison my son's mind,' she yelled at me. 'I got him back from Chicago—he will live with me.' I was dismayed. His father wouldn't even talk to me; I was an outsider to them, and they treated me as such. I did feel sorry for Mohan, he was caught between his mother and me. When we were alone, he placated me, but whenever his mother was around, he endorsed her whims and misgivings. At first, all this was just simmering tension, but later it became unbearable. Besides, it was her overflowing delight whenever Mohan took her side, which made me so uneasy. Despondently, I settled into what Obaasan had called *the routines of married life*: religious rituals, rustic rules, and rude remonstrations—such were the *alliterations of routine*, a reverse of freedom, nothing more than an unchanging life. Each morning was the same, every evening no different. My sole solace was escaping through work.

I worked at the branch office of the Bombay newspaper and tried to be out of the house for as long as I possibly could. In those few stolen hours, before and after work, I returned to my self—I *was* myself. But when I was home, I couldn't recognise the person I had become—I wasn't me. I restored myself now and then by living a dream. I tried to see through the eyes of that little girl, sunlight trickling through the leaves. The grass was lush, the wind crisp, and flowers bloomed all around her, me.

My aunt had been pleased that Mohan and I were to be married but I could tell my uncle was not; he didn't stop me, though, and instead, he said, 'Be sure this is what you want. After all, life is also about what happens when you make mistakes.' I hadn't grasped the implications of his words at the time, but now, I understood. I had trustingly imagined life—its entirety, its various phases—being somewhat in harmony. 'Life's like music, there are different notes: both high and low,' my uncle had once told me. All I could hear now was an all-encompassing silence—a disquieting gap in the music, unchanging, and flowless. Every time I called my uncle, he asked me the same question: *How are you?* I could feel the weight of his query. *I'm fine*, I would say, and I'm certain he felt the heaviness of my replies. He didn't probe, and I didn't confide.

I got pregnant a year later. I was overjoyed, and so were Mohan and his mother. She fussed over me, stopped me from going to work. 'It's not healthy for my grandson,' she said, 'you must rest.' Of course, Mohan agreed with her, but I didn't listen to either of them. Matters only got worse when I miscarried eighteen weeks later. 'You've killed my grandson,' my mother-in-law wept. It was too early to tell the sex of the child: would they have been a girl or a boy?

Mohan looked broken when I told him I was leaving, as though each part of his body had been twisted and bent; pain oozed from his eyes.

It was raining the day I left, just as it had been on the day I arrived. My uncle gathered me in his arms; my heart was pounding against his chest. The thunderous rain, momentarily obliterating all that was.

* * *

In the two years I was away in Bangalore, my uncle had retired from his work. He was now a consultant to the Wool Traders Association and was home most of the time; my aunt wasn't. With Malli's help, she had bought a plot of land in Sarmoli and frequently went to the village to supervise the building of the house. Upon my return, I resumed work in the newspaper office. S-san's cards and gifts still came regularly, and I spoke to her every now and then; I missed her and Tokyo, and the time we spent together in the city. I had applied to several magazines in Tokyo for a job, I told her, but hadn't heard from any of them.

S-san called late one night and told me about a French girl who lived in Sakura House who worked at the Asia Research Centre. S-san had spoken to the head of the centre, who had told her that despite there being many foreigners at the centre, there had been no Indians. S-san urged me to write to him, and so I sent him a letter the next morning. He replied a few weeks later: *We would be happy to have you*, he wrote. I called S-san and told her the good news. 'I will need a room,' I said.

She replied, 'You can stay with me.'

'Nan wo tenzuru—' S-san said and held me close '*—problems which turn for the better*.' Nothing more was asked or said about my marriage or lost child. Time, like the waves, receded again. From my bedroom window, I could see the one-foot-by-one-foot window of the dormitory kitchen; it was shut tight.

I had some time before joining the research centre, so I arranged to meet Akiko at the Saké Art House. She looked well, had put on some weight. I noticed she didn't have a plaster on, and when I asked her about it, she said, 'I'm so happy. I'm pregnant. You remember Takagi-san, whom you saw the first time we met? He's the father. I don't need a plaster now I have this.' She gently patted her belly with her hand. 'Now tell me about you. What have you been doing since we last met?'

I told her as briefly as I could. 'I'm so sorry,' she said. 'Be tough. Be a zakuro.' I told her about my village and the photo exhibition I had in Bombay. 'You should exhibit your photos here—I will arrange it for you.' And she did.

I saw Yasunari. He had grown a beard, though not much of one. 'I needed a change,' he said, 'after Hiroo and I split. He moved to Paris; he's joined his mother's firm.' He laughed, but his eyes revealed a deeper truth. 'I'm so busy these days, I have no time for relationships,' he said, 'or shaving.'

I travelled to Kyoto to see Obaasan. She had transformed the new house into a shibori museum and workshop and now lived with Katayama-san in a rented house down the street; oddly, Ojiisan had built the house. 'Ojiisan lives here with me,' she said.

I went to the bank where Ryu had worked; he had left, the manager told me, had moved to America, but he didn't know where. He had to do what he had to do when he had to do it, I thought.

I started work at the research centre; it was hectic, and for this, I was glad. I travelled to many different parts of Japan, and though my colleagues went overseas—to distant places, to collect stories—I couldn't go with them, my boss told me, as it was only my first year. One day as I was in the research centre's library going through back issues of *National Geographic*—the centre contributed stories to it—I was surprised and thrilled when I came across a photo essay by Ryu. He had found his oku at last, and I was happy for him. I wrote to the magazine and asked them to send me his address and heard back from him some months later: he was in San Francisco. His father had died, and his mother had returned to her village. *You have to visit*, he wrote, *it's a marvellous city*.

Although we had separated, Mohan and I remained friends and wrote to each other regularly. He was back in Chicago now, said he couldn't deal with his mother's ways anymore. He had a girlfriend: Valeria, a Mexican American, she was nice, though very Catholic. I wondered what his mother would say about that.

I heard from my uncle and aunt, but not often. They were busy with the house construction in Sarmoli, it was nearly complete, and they would be moving there soon.

By the end of the year, Akiko had arranged an exhibition of my photos. I also got a call from the editor of a photo journal some days later. She told me they were planning an issue on conflict that would portray places devastated by war, terrorism, militancy, and that they would like to include a feature on Kashmir.

'I want you to write your own story,' the editor said. 'You said you were six when you had to leave your village. Do you remember what happened?'

'Of course,' I replied. 'I remember it all.'

* * *

It's been over a year since I joined the research centre in Tokyo. I took some weeks off from work to go to Sarmoli. Malli wept when she saw me; it was the first time I had seen her cry like that. I felt my pain in her pain. She held me close, and I could feel her heart throbbing against mine.

She comes to me now, sits beside me. The Panchachuli mountains are shrouded in darkness. I turn my head, but the mountains arouse no emotions within me. They seem to be utterly indifferent to me and somewhat ominous, foreboding. I am seized by unease; gloom fills my mind. I think of all the people I knew who had died: my parents, Arun, Tatha and Patti, Ojiisan, and, most of all, my child. I had immersed myself in work, kept busy the past few years, but thoughts of my child come to me more clearly now. I wanted a girl: her eyes, her nose and rounded mouth, her clenched little fingers, her folded limbs, all float distinctly before my eyes. She was a part of me, was tied to me. I had a name for her, Shizuka—*quiet*. She is soundless in the womb of my heart, and all I can feel is a void. I sigh, long and deep. If I were to change, will all that surrounds me cease to sustain? Or if my surroundings were to alter, would I cease to be who I am? In this moment, I feel a fierce compulsion to flee—even if only for a short while—from myself. I remind myself of Matsumoto-san's words: 'You need to do but two things: believe and dream.'

Malli grabs my turbid thoughts in the warmth of her

hand, and as she always has, she dispels them bit by bit. She is an irreplaceable friend, her bright spirit, constitutionally devoid of angst or sadness, is powerfully resilient. She can translate my tumultuous feelings for me; transform them into a calming silence. 'Don't think about all that has passed,' she says, 'go with the flow.' Her pragmatic manner infects me, and as I feel my hand in hers, my forlorn thoughts wilt. I recollect what the monk in Kamakura had said about Zen: 'To move, go with the flow, because in the end, there will be nothing but a void, after which there will be a new beginning. It is a new beginning for me, and I will move on.'

Moonlight shines on my face and the potted desert rose beside me. 'I will leave it in the pot,' my aunt had said, 'maybe it prefers it this way.' Perhaps it did, perhaps I did. I know I preferred to be safe in the shell I had built around me. It contained a world inhabited by my parents, Arun, my aunt and uncle, Malli, S-san, a few close friends, and Shizuka.

I pluck a fallen blossom of the desert rose: candy pink on its edges, milky white in the middle, and yellow deep within. I examine it thoroughly, detail by detail. I remember the day my father took me to the top of a hill, and we looked down at the meadows, the curling river, the forest of trees, and the brilliant sky above. 'Look, Kavya, so beautiful. Nothing on earth can be as lovely as this,' he told me. 'Each part is like a note of music. Close your eyes, and you will hear its song.' He was a simple farmer, but he possessed a clear idea of beauty: fresh dew on the flowers, spiderwebs, the light-lined clouds, the sun rising over the hills, a pair of eyes. Even though I was very young, with a few simple words, he made me understand that a thing is beautiful only when everything in it fits, and you can touch it with the fingers of your heart.

I hold the desert rose bloom up against the backdrop of the mountains. It is alluring, giving no false guarantee of beauty and is such a pretty flower: whorl upon whorl, part growing from part, consuming every bit of vigour and spirit. Now I understand that true beauty is to be found not in the thing itself, like this flower, or the cherry blossoms that fade away in a matter of days, but in the process that has made it beautiful: the toil, the joy, and the passage from one moment to another. Another place. Another time. Another season.

It is summer now. When I told S-san I was going to Sarmoli, she said, 'I want to see the Himalayas, can I come with you?' She had brought the desert rose for my aunt, had hidden it in her suitcase. It was one foot tall, and its knotted roots were wrapped in mud and wires, a discarded plastic pouch, and covered with an old Japanese newspaper.

She comes to me now, sits down beside me. My uncle and aunt join us. We don't speak—our minds are vacant, are tsurezure-ing. My aunt reaches out and holds S-san's hand. My heart's fingers touch the warmth of the breeze. It is now truly dark, but even in the dimness, I feel the beauty of the mountains. I close my eyes, hear its song.

Author's Note

My father joined the Indian National Army in Tokyo, an armed force formed by Indian nationalists and Imperial Japan during World War II. It sought to fight for India's independence from British colonial rule. When I was little, my father sang their marching song—*kadam kadam badaye ja*—like a lullaby. He told me stories about the war, the bombing of Hiroshima, and how when planes rained their bombs down on Tokyo, he would rush to his radio station to broadcast to his fellow countrymen. When I asked him why he risked his life, he replied, *To free the country I love*. By the time I was born, my country was already free; therefore, I couldn't understand the people who fought in wars, who sacrificed their lives and the lives of their loved ones for a country. To the contrary, I grew up in many different cities across India and never lived anywhere long enough to call home.

My father had studied at Tokyo University and hoped I would as well—I did, but I was alone, an outsider. I didn't belong. I didn't know the language at first except for *goodbye*, *thank you*, *please*, and *excuse me*, and so, I resorted to listening and seeing instead of speaking. I went on long bus and train rides, and I was often lost. In the years I spent in Tokyo, a new world opened out before me—of refined aesthetics and subtle sensibilities and of Zen. For this, I will always be grateful to my father.

Now my parents are both dead, and my roots are gone. All I have left now are my children and grandchildren, but they are not my roots; I am theirs. I know now that belonging is as precious as love, that it precedes it.

The characters in this small book are homeless, lost in many different ways, some for only a short time, others much longer. I relate to them; I live through them. And I am grateful to them. In their stories, I found shelter—a home.

My appreciations go to Michelle Tudor of Platypus Press—she read every draft of the book and offered invaluable suggestions. For this and her meticulous editing, I am thankful. She knew the story I wanted to tell and helped me tell it.

About the Author

Sarayu Srivatsa trained as an architect and city planner at the Madras and Tokyo universities. She was a professor of architecture at Bombay University, the editor of the *Indian Architect* and *Builder Review*, and has written extensively on the evolution and growth of cities. Her book, *Where the Streets Lead*, was published in 1997 and won the JIIA Award.

She also co-authored two books with the late poet and writer Dom Moraes: *The Long Strider*, part-biography, part-travelogue, tells the extraordinary story of Thomas Coryate; and *Out of God's Oven* (shortlisted for the Kiriyama Prize), a vivid discussion—based on personal memories and first-hand accounts—examining the deep divides still present in modern-day India.

Her first novel, *The Last Pretence*, was longlisted for the Man Asian Literary Prize, and upon its release in the UK (under the title *If You Look For Me, I am Not Here*), was also included on *The Guardian*'s Not the Booker Prize longlist.

She lives in Mumbai and has a son and daughter and three granddaughters, Rosa, Lola, and Tara.

Platypus Press, est. 2015 · England · platypuspress.co.uk